3/17

Also by Sam Shepard

The One Inside

The One Inside

Sam Shepard

Foreword by Patti Smith

Alfred A. Knopf, New York 2017

For

Patti Lee

Roxanne and Sandy

Walker and Hannah

Jesse and Maura

Why does no one take you aside and tell you what is coming?

—*David Foster Wallace*

Foreword

There were four horses grazing beyond the fence, black butterflies alighting on the fallen pears. You could already feel the approach of autumn, a golden Kentucky afternoon. Sam was looking out the window. I was at the table reading his manuscript.

Glancing up at him, it occurred to me that everything I ever knew of Sam, and he of me, was still inside us. I thought of a photograph of the two of us in New York City, walking past an automat on Twenty-third Street, some forty years ago. It was shot from behind, but it was us, without question, about to embark on separate paths that would surely cross again.

The manuscript before me is a dark compass. All points proceed from its magnetic north—the interior landscape of the narrator. Unable to tear myself away I read straight through the afternoon, navigating a mosaic of echoing conversations, altered perspectives, lucid memory, and hallucinatory impressions.

The narrator awakes in the midst of a rude metamorphosis. Coordinates are shuffled, but the hand is familiar. He's been an actor for most of his adult life, enabling a kind of travel that requires no passport, just a truck, script, and his dogs on the scent of nostalgia.

The smells of donuts, steam, waffles, and coffee spilled out across the busted-up yard and into the vast dark desert.

Foreword

Speechless men hauled huge heavy boxes on iron wheels across the gravel. Now and then, one of the forms would emit a nod or a groan, but the world remained enigmatic, shrouded, and unspeakable.

He has dreams of his father, *the tiny man* who was not so tiny. He describes the minutiae of these recurring dreams with haunting hilarity, reminiscent of Japanese manga comics. He attempts to run, separate himself from his father and all his indiscretions, but is condemned to repeat them. Time frames; the faces of women meld into one another. His father's young lover, Felicity, and her mouthy mother in a pink coat. The too young, ambitious, and elusive Blackmail Girl. His wife of thirty years driving away. They come and go and return again. After a while you get to know them, their images intricately fabricated through fast-moving prose, liberal smatterings of poetry, monologue, and dialogue. The visceral language of flickering home movies.

He loves his wife but they just can't get along. He's beguiled by the Blackmail Girl who is something of himself, testing and weighing reactions. Circling back in time, he collides with his younger self, naively entwined with his father's Felicity, a tragic character pulled like taffy, vacillating between innocence and desire.

Her mouth opened and I saw tiny animals escaping: tiny animals trapped inside her all this time. They flew out as though something might catch them and drag them back into imprisonment. I could feel them land on my face and crawl through my hair, searching for a hiding place. Each time she screamed the animals flew out in small clouds like tiny gnats: little drag-ons, flying fish, headless horses.

Throughout life he is captivated, confused, and amused by women, drawn toward them yet compelled to skip out. But in the end it's not so much about the women as the shifting core of the narrator. We travel the coils of his prismatic mind, his weary heart, not through confession, but a potent honesty, a fascination for not caring. The truth is that he may be chang-ing, yet he remains unchanged, the running boy, the empow-ered adolescent, the seething man whose muscles betray him.

He's a loner who doesn't want to be alone, grappling with the incubus, a rippling of nocturnal waters, the nausea of unending nights. There are troubling moments of prescience, as he intu-its future fragmentation, stoically kicking his way through the shards. He's just going to keep on living till he dies. Whether he paints himself in a good or bad light is not the point. The point is to lay stuff out, smooth the curling edges.

I set down the manuscript. It's him, sort of him, not him at all. It's an entity trying to break out, make sense of things. A tapeworm slithering from the stomach, through the open mouth, down the bedsheets, straight into the bleak infinite.

You are now traveling. Your future is frozen. Rapidly, you are jettisoned from the blank unknown to the bright clear world.

I notice the light has changed, a burnished twilight that quickly ushers us into the night. I get up to examine an image that Sam had tacked, slightly askew, in a niche above the kitchen sink. A madman woman shaman with a boom box.

—Where was that taken?

—Somewhere in the Sonora desert.

—Is it real?

Maybe, he says, but who knows what is real anyway.

Reality is overrated. What remains are the words scrawled upon an unwinding panorama, vestiges of dusty stills peeled from memory, a threnody of gone voices drifting across the American plain. *The One Inside* is a coalescing atlas, marked by the boot heels of one who instinctively tramps, with open eyes, the stretches of its unearthly roads.

—Patti Smith

The One Inside

The One Inside

They've murdered something far off. Fighting over it. Yes. Screaming. Doing their mad cackle as they tear into its softness. He's awake—5:05 a.m. Pitch black. Distant coyotes. Must've been. He's awake, in any case. Staring at rafters. Adjusting to "place." Awake, even after a full Xanax, in anticipation of small demons—horses with human heads. All small, as though life-size were too big to fathom. His dogs are on the muscle, howling from the kitchen in feral imitation. Vicious cold again. Blue snow biting at the windowsills: glowing in what's left of the full moon. He throws the blankets back with a bullfighter's flourish and swings both bony knees out into the raw air. He comes, almost immediately, to a straight-backed sitting position, both hands flat on his thighs. He tries to take in the ever-changing landscape of his body—where he resides? Which part? He peers down at his very thick, blue, thermal hiking socks, pilfered from some movie set. Piece of some costume—some character, long forgotten. They've come and gone, these characters, like brief, violent love affairs: trailers— honey wagons—morning burritos—craft service tents—phony limousines—hot towels—4 a.m. calls. Forty-some years of it. Too big. Hard to believe. Too vast. How did I get in here? His aluminum trailer rocks and sways in the howling Chinooks.

His young face staring back at him through a cheap 4 x 4 mirror, surrounded by bare light bulbs. Outside, they're shooting film of grasshoppers, falling in great swirling cones from the belly of a rented helicopter. They actually are. In the background— winter wheat, as big around as your thumb, blows in rolling waves.

Now, perched on the very edge of his firm mattress, staring down at his thick blue socks, white puffs of breath vaporizing in the morning dark, he knows it's all come true. He just sits like that for a while—straight-backed. A great blue heron waiting for a frog to rise.

The house doesn't creak; it's made of concrete. Outside, the aspens moan. He doesn't feel the cold now. It crosses his mind that it's been over two years since the very sudden breakup with his last wife. A woman he'd been with for almost thirty years. *Crosses his mind.* Pictures. The source? "Am I whining now?" he asks himself, in the voice of a small boy. A boy he remembers, but not him. Not this one, now, quaking in blue thermal socks.

6:00 a.m.: Wind just now quit after furious blowing out of the south, for three days straight. Air still and much warmer. House even feels hot. Thought—today I'm exactly one year older than my father was when he died. Weird thought, as though it were some kind of achievement rather than raw chance. Rather than happenstance. Pull off black silk long-handles. Female. Electric-blue crackles of static. I see sparks shooting from my chest. Electricity is in me. Take the many pills prescribed by acupuncturist. Line them all up. Colors. Shapes. Sizes. Don't even know what they're for. Just do what you're told. Somebody must know something. Do what you're told. First light cracks through the piñons. Dogs, dead asleep on the kitchen floor, splayed out like they were caught suspended in a gallop. Make coffee in old stained pot. Dump yesterday's grounds. Mice rustling in heat vents, searching for warmth. Thinking about Nabokov's answer to why he writes— *"aesthetic bliss"*—that's all—"aesthetic bliss." Yes. Whatever that means.

Tiny Man

Early morning: They deliver my father's corpse in the trunk of a '49 Mercury coupe, dew still heavy on the taillights. His body is wrapped up tight in see-through plastic, head to toe. Flesh-colored rubber bands bind it at the neck, waist, and ankles—mummy style. He's become very small in the course of things—maybe eight inches tall. In fact, I'm holding him now, in the palm of my hand. I ask them for permission to unwrap his tiny head, just to make sure he's truly dead. They allow me to do this. They all stand aside, hands clasped behind their tailored backs, heads bowed in a kind of ashamed mourning but not something you would question them on. It's smart to keep on their good side. Besides, they seem quite polite and stoic now.

The Mercury idles with a deep penetrating rumble I can feel through the soles of both shoes. I remove the rubber bands carefully and uncover his face, peeling the Saran Wrap away from his nose very slowly. It makes a sticky sound like linoleum coming free from its glue. His mouth opens involuntarily—some delayed response of the nervous system, no doubt, but I take it as a last gasp. I put my thumb inside and feel his rough gums. Little ripples where his teeth used to be. He had no teeth in life, either—the life I remember him in. I re-wrap his head in the plastic sheathing, replace the rubber bands, and hand him back over, thanking them all with a slight nod, trying to stay in keeping with the solemnity of things. They take him carefully from me and place him back in the dark trunk with the other miniatures. There are shrunken women wedged on either side of him retaining all their alluring features in perfect detail: high cheekbones, eyebrows plucked, lashes caked in blue mascara, hair washed and coifed, smelling like ripe cane sugar. His is the only tiny body that faces completely out toward a band of sunlight. When they close the trunk this band goes to black, as though a cloud has abruptly covered the sun.

They stand in a semicircle facing me now, hands clasped over their groins, casually yet formally. I can't tell if they're ex-Marines or mobsters. They seem a mixture of both. I salute each one, rotating counterclockwise. I have the impression that some even click their heels, fascist style, but I may be making this up. I don't know if this rain just started or if it's been going on for some time. I watch them drive off in a light drizzle.

That's about all I can remember. Along with these smattered details is a strange morning grief, but of what, I can't say.

Felicity

In another language, in another time, her name meant "happiness," I guess. "Felicity," I think it was—"Felicity"—yes, that was it. I'd never heard that name before—like from an English novel. Very young. Freckle faced. Red hair. Slightly plump. Adolescent. Always wearing simple cotton one-piece dresses that looked homemade. She'd scream like a trapped rabbit when she sat backward on my father's cock. I'd never heard such ecstasy and horror, all at once. I'd listen from the next room, staring at the ceiling. Something smelled like eucalyptus and Vaseline. They never talked. I'd listen. But they never talked. I'd dare myself to go in there, just go in and appear and don't say a thing. Just stare like some zombie child—a child who just shows up from out of nowhere. What could they do? Stare back. Kick me out? Put on clothes and kick me out? I knew what they were doing, I knew it felt good. I knew it must feel good to be inside another person. Deep inside like that.

I went in and there she was. My father's girlfriend sitting ramrod straight—naked almost—as though she were riding a pony backward. Neither of them noticed me. They never turned to see me. She just kept on riding him and screaming recklessly, working her way up and down in a frenzy. He was on his back on a table, staring at the ceiling, his arms folded behind his head, like he might be taking a siesta or listening to the radio. His lips were moving but nothing came out. I walked right up next to them but they never turned to see me. Her pink underwear were on the floor. They looked like they belonged to an older woman, maybe her mother.

There was a frantic knocking and banging at the door but neither of them paid any attention. Felicity just kept screaming and pumping away. Sometimes she would lean slightly forward, look down, and examine the penetration closely, without passion. Her mouth was open wide and her hair stuck to the sweat on her forehead. The knocking and banging went on. I went to the door and cracked it. I had my jockey shorts and T-shirt on. It was Mabel Hynes, the landlady, from down the hall. She stood there with a Mexican hairless in the folds of her flabby arms. The dog was silent but kept its ears pricked for each scream. When the scream came, the dog yapped.

"What's going on in there? Sounds like someone's getting murdered."

"No, it's just my dad."

"Your dad? What's he doing?"

"Just having fun. He's got a friend with him."

"Fun? Doesn't sound like fun to me."

"I've never seen her before, actually. This girl."

"Yeah, well, tell him if he doesn't find a way to keep the noise down, I'm calling the cops."

"Okay."

"You tell him that."

"Okay."

"I've got enough to worry about without his shenanigans."

"Yes, ma'am."

I closed the door and bolted it. Felicity kept on, but now her screams became short little cries of mercy. My father stayed silent. Maybe his lips kept moving. He was always moving his lips as though talking to someone invisible. They still didn't seem to know I was there. I pulled on my jeans and snuck out the back door, barefoot.

It was cold when I hit the ground. Just getting dawn. Behind our rooming house was a long black rail yard going off to Stanley and Bingham. It diminished into blinking neon and brakeman's signals. They were loading secret metals that someone told me were being sent out to Los Alamos and Alamogordo. The cargo were hissing and groaning as they waited. The smells of donuts, steam, waffles, and coffee spilled out across the busted-up yard and into the vast dark desert. Speechless men hauled huge heavy boxes on iron wheels across the gravel. Now and then, one of the forms would emit a nod or a groan, but the world remained enigmatic, shrouded, and unspeakable.

I followed the same rules of geographic orientation as if I were walking alongside a quiet river. On the way out I would keep the tracks on my left shoulder, and on my way back keep them on my right. Long as I used the tracks to guide me, I'd never get lost. Simple. I followed the long iron snake until the commercial lights of downtown receded to dots. My steps became louder. Lizards and little animals darted away. I tried to keep to the smooth cool sand but bullthorns and shattered bottles tortured my bare feet. Little soft patches of cooch grass gave me momentary respite until some thorn or nail punched through and finally I had to retreat. The iron rail still held heat from the day before and I found myself hopping back to town on the creosoted ties.

Once I reentered the nest of pink neon and green beer ads I looked for a light in the window of our boarding room. I imagined I saw it from that distance. I imagined I saw my dad frying bacon but maybe not. Maybe I was making something up. A solid life of uncertainty.

Squad cars surrounded the rooming house. Swirling blue lights. Mrs. Hynes was standing on the front porch surveying the goings-on with her little dog yapping in her arms and a sweater thrown over her shoulders against the early-morning chill. She had the grim look of someone watching the aftermath of a road accident. Felicity was standing on the sidewalk wearing a sheet, teeth chattering, sobbing, as a female officer tried to keep the top of the sheet closed tightly around Felicity's huge breasts. Purple mascara ran down her cheeks. The lady cop escorted her into one of the squad cars, which immediately sped off with its siren wailing. A woman in a long pink coat was yelling at my father, who was in his boxer shorts, smoking a cigarette. A cop stood on either side of him, squeezing on his bare elbows, then handcuffed his wrists behind his back. The woman in the pink coat kept yelling things like "Cocksucker!" and "Bastard!" while the cops placed him in the back seat of another squad car and protected the top of his head from hitting the doorframe. Which I thought was a really strange gesture since they were already doing severe damage to his character. Now, all the police cars sped off with their sirens screaming, following my father as though he'd just shot the president. Mrs. Hynes went back inside with her dog and shut off the porch light. The woman in the long pink coat kept crying and going in little circles, searching through her deep pockets for more crumpled Kleenex. Her lips were moving. She was talking to someone far away. She bent down and took off both her high heels. She dangled them from one finger as she weaved away from me, down Trace Street.

Purple as Blue

You know what it is, don't you? It's the blue mascara. Why that color, for instance? Blue? Crying? Why crying? You asked for it. It was you all along. I told you—mess with an older man, you're asking for trouble. I told you that and you didn't believe me, did you? Why else would you go out and buy blue mascara? Deliberately. Why would you hang around? He's an older man. I told you and you didn't believe me, did you.

Castles in the Moonlight

She simply walked out on me, this last one—not Felicity—(I'll think up a suitable name for her later), this young Girl—let's call her that for now. Not the "wife" or "wives," as it were, but another one, extremely young, for my age, that is. Something in me can't quite believe it. Anyway, one bright morning there she was, like an apparition from the forties, standing at attention with her red Naugahyde suitcase ready to roll. Point-blank. In the kitchen, too, before I'd even had a shot of coffee, she told me in a sort of whispered monotone that she thought she was "leading me on." That was her phrase, like something disconnected to her essence was somehow seducing me beyond her volition. Some ghost of herself. I found it a little hard to believe and began flailing around in my short memory for some other clue, some transgression I might have committed at the breakfast table. In any case, I put up no big objection—the more I protested, the more convinced she might become. She told me she was going off to see her aunt in San Francisco. Some "aunt"—flying that very morning. "Adios." I lost what little composure I could summon and asked her why this sudden departure when we hadn't even had time to settle in. She told me it had to do with my polishing off more than half an ornate bottle of mescal the night before, including the ropy worm, and plunging into long rambling associations of joint suicides from the medieval past, mainly Heinrich von Kleist and his young mistress, Henriette, on the banks of a gigantic lake lapping softly through the night while the little German town in the distance slept soundly. No lights. Just the distant silhouettes of castles in the moonlight. Maybe this could all be true. Her huge brown eyes were full of conviction. We are from totally different eras, after all. Time has marooned us, without feeling.

Succubus

Another morning, before this Girl came along, something was crouched on my chest—curled up there like a cat, but it wasn't. I awoke very cautiously, careful not to disturb the creature, barely breathing for fear the thing might spring at my face. Maybe some kind of phantom or—succubus, is that what they call it? In any case, the One who distributes destinies and nightmares, That One. Female, for sure. Curled up like it was the warmest place in the house, eyes focused on the wall above—yellow eyes—posing for someone taking a picture of her with an iPhone, maybe. She wore a leering grin like one of those cat demons in a Goya drawing that seem without motivation. Black eyes, Pacino dead eyes. I didn't feel panic but I could feel all the signals of alarm going off inside me. Little electric jolts through my shoulder and ears. Stinging with "prickly heat." I watched her down the length of my nose without moving my head. I didn't try to touch her or shoo her away. I wanted no sudden hysterics; no thrashing around that might turn into accidental slashing or biting. A deep throbbing drone came from her neck, but still this was unlike any domestic cat I'd ever come across. I remembered seeing a rare strip of black-and-white footage, taken maybe in the twenties, of the last captured Tasmanian devil before that species became extinct (or has it?), but it was unlike that monster as well. Not as big. No stripe. This was simply a lurking presence that happened to inhabit a feline shape. I just watched for a long, long time as she slowly rotated her head from left to right, then, I suppose, she'd had enough of whatever warmth I was emanating and slunk off, weasel-like, dissolving into the folds of the hallway. I lay still for a while, feeling cold drafts sift through the room. I listened to the thermostat click over. Not moving seemed important. Maybe I had turned to stone.

Blackmail Dialogue

"I've been recording all our phone conversations, you know."

"What?"

"All these years. Yup."

"With a tape recorder, you mean? Like a detective?"

"Well—"

"How long? We haven't known each other that long."

"A long, long time."

"Oh God."

"There's nothing to be ashamed of. They're very beautiful."

"What are? No—"

"The conversations."

"What are you going to do with them?"

"Put them in a book."

"A book?"

"By me."

"By you?"

"By me."

"What about me?"

"All right, coauthored by you and me, then."

"I don't want to be a part of this!"

"I've already got them typed up."

"Oh no!"

"'They're beautiful! You've said some beautiful things over the years."

"'No, I haven't. I've said nothing beautiful! Nothing I've said is of any importance."

"'You have."

"'It hasn't been years, either."

"'Over the one year, then."

"'What, for instance?"

"'All the descriptions of my pussy."

"'No!"

"'All the stuff about your penis."

"'No, no, no, no, no."

"'The way it stands up and throbs and gets all juicy."

"Listen—"

"My pussy and your penis—beautiful!"

"Oh God—NO!"

"Yes."

"Why? Who would be interested?"

"Plenty of people."

"No! No one."

"You said my pussy was like a pomegranate, for instance."

"No, I didn't! I never said that!"

"'Multifaceted,' you called it."

"NO!"

"Multifaceted and ubiquitous."

"Ubiquitous?"

"It goes on forever. All at once."

"Stop!"

"No—"

"Please stop!"

"My pussy will go on forever! All at once. That's what you said. Do you want to meet up and I'll show them to you?"

"What?"

"The conversations."

"You've got them all written down? Hard copy?"

"Of course."

"No."

"No, what?"

"No meeting. I want you to stay as far away from me as possible."

"But why?"

"Your age, for one thing. How old are you, anyway?"

"Very young."

"That's what I thought."

"No one cares."

"Everyone cares. It's illegal."

"Why are you so afraid of breaking the law?"

"*You're* the one who should be afraid of the law."

"I haven't done anything wrong."

"Oh no? Plagiarism?"

"What's that?"

"To pass someone else's work off as your own."

"It's both of ours."

"It's not! It's neither! It's not even work. It's talk."

"There are some beautiful things in there—beautiful moments."

"There's nothing in there of any intention."

"Sometimes the most beautiful things are purely accidental."

"That stuff was never intended to be recorded, let alone written down! Plagiarism is what it is. Pure and simple."

Famous Golfer

I wonder what finally drove her to make this call? There's no doubt she'd been thinking about it for some time. Plotting. She'd made her mind up to confront me with it. The idea that our casual conversation might have some merit—even literary value. The whole thing was outrageous. Why? "Ambition" was easy to come up with, but did she really think it was that easy? A nineteen-year-old girl? What made her first think it up? Maybe it was my invitation for her to stay in my guest room. It could have been that. Little did I know. When I was nineteen, I certainly had ambition, but I wanted to be a famous golfer, not a literary figure. I didn't want to be nearly as famous as, say, Arnold Palmer, Jack Nicklaus, or Gary Player or any of the ten best back then. I simply wanted to be on the professional tour and in the hunt. One of those young guns who's always threatening but just not "there" yet. A great putter and chipper. (I was known for my short game.) The literary world was way over my head anyway. Mailer, Capote, Nabokov. How would you ever begin a conversation with one of those nuts? I know nothing about butterflies, hand-to-hand combat, or whisperings of the Deep South. Maybe she just wanted to be associated with me. Maybe she thought she could just short-circuit all the toil and sweat and jump right to the juicy stuff: bright lights, Tony Awards, limos with Russian drivers who don't speak English. Wouldn't it be great if you could just wish yourself to be famous—like you had some genie at your command? It didn't matter what your "artistic state" was— whether you had something to "say" or not—whether or not you had an ax to grind, politically or otherwise. You just one day wind up famous and that's that. Look—I'm famous! Can you see me glitter? Can you see my spangles? I don't deserve it, but then, who does?

Early Anthropology

Last night he was struggling on brittle knees to light a fire. He remembers. He remembers that much. Lighting stick matches to balls of crumpled outdated obituaries from *The New York Times* (he still had the habit of dipping into the Sunday section now and then). Blazing piñon and cedar while she sat, propped up on his leather couch with her taut knees sticking out and running on about Android Genocide, Virtual Videos, Driverless Google Trucks, Collective Mind Particles, Dolphin Vision—things like that. Running them all together loosely, end on end, in a kind of tapestry of association that he found bewildering to follow. He nodded acknowledgment, pretending to track her train of thought while watching an early anthropologist's face flare up in flames. Some guy who once discovered an unheard-of tribe in New Guinea back in the distant sixties—untouched by European influence. Wild, naked people, running around with spears, attacking neighbors—raiding, pillaging, kidnapping, killing at random. Coming at the time it did, this discovery was concurrent with the Tet Offensive, which seemed to be the only issue of real importance back then—monks going up in blue flames, pistols point-blank to the head, orange serpent napalm waves erupting through the jungle. Turns out, through further studies by this extinguished scientist, the cannibals' entire motivation was simply to acquire young females. *Girls.* That was what was behind all this. Girls.

In any case, I wasn't trying to suggest that she and I should try joint suicide. I hardly even know her. Just take guns and blast each other's brains out. That's ridiculous.

Sheet of White Paper

Finally, desperately, I told her I was ready to make a deal. I didn't feel so old, I just looked old, I told her. I looked slightly ridiculous in my thermal socks, too, I admitted that. She made no gesture of recognition. Kept her head low. Mute. I'd just come out of a long relationship of insipid stalemate and now, I said, negotiation seemed appealing. She could go ahead and fly to San Francisco to visit this "aunt" of hers (there was nothing I could do about it anyway), but then, if she decided to come back, I promised no more agave and I would completely refrain from any mention of suicide—joint or otherwise. I wasn't begging, either. She told me she would consider it but she was definitely going. I nodded. She'd had enough. "Fine," I said, "that's all I'm looking for—that's all I want—a little consideration." She almost smiled. "Just do me one kind favor and return the rental car to the rental place down off the highway. We'll definitely stay in touch." Again, no answer. I made no attempt to even peck her paternally on the forehead. She took off in the early-morning mist in some front-wheel-drive Japanese job, looking very small behind the wheel.

I went on about my business, although rattled. My hands shook. I kept everything in and resisted the sensation that aloneness brings sometimes—to let everything out. I did my usual stuff after she left, although her eyes kept popping up in front of me. Her huge brown eyes. I poured coffee into my favorite cup that said "Weed, California" on one side, a red bucking horse on the other. I sat at the little Mexican table, looking out at birds feeding on black-oil sunflower seeds. Juncos scratching then stopping abruptly, listening as though to something they'd never heard before. Now and then, the giant scrub jay would sweep in and take over, causing all the little ones to flee, just like those helpless villagers in a Kurosawa film. I remember asking her one morning if she'd ever heard of Kurosawa. She hadn't. I was not surprised.

I pulled myself together by doing some arm and shoulder exercises I'd learned from a theater director. The landline rang, and it was her again. I was glad to hear her kid-like voice. She was at the car rental place and couldn't find the drop box for the ignition key. I imagined her standing there by the side of the highway, the key dangling from one finger. Her waist. It was still early and the place wasn't open yet. I asked her how she was going to get to the airport from there and she said some boyfriend was going to pick her up and drive her. "Some boyfriend?" I said.

"Oh, here it is. I found it. Never mind." Evidently, she'd just discovered the key drop. "I'll call you from San Francisco," she said, and hung up.

I decided to take the little red beat-up Tacoma down to have breakfast at Manny's Roadhouse, then pick up a load of dry cedar for the kitchen chiminayo. I like the redness of cedar and the way it smells once you've got it roaring. At first, I thought the truck wasn't going to turn over in this sudden cold snap but it turns out I hadn't pressed the clutch all the way to the floor. One of those safety devices built into the ignition system in case you're dumb enough to start it in gear. I left the dogs to roam on their own and took off down the frozen dirt road. Ravens were pulling the stringy guts out of a squashed rabbit and seemed very reluctant to get out of the way. I didn't slow down.

At Manny's, I took a counter stool next to the turquoise wall at the very end of the row so at least I wouldn't have anyone sitting to the immediate right of me. I like reading in public places, especially at breakfast. It's a way of cutting myself off from having to make small talk and, at the same time, diving deeply into a world of fiction. It's a way of cutting yourself off completely, in fact. I set down my copy of Bruno Schulz's *Sanatorium Under the Sign of the Hourglass*—a very rare edition. I think the Girl had ordered it for me through Amazon or eBay or something. Hardbound—full of Bruno's own illustrations. His own drawings. Bruno was an odd little Polish Jew with a very large head, apparently, from the looks of his self-portraits. A schoolteacher who taught drawing and basic mathematics but also wrote extraordinary florid prose in his spare time—which he didn't have much of, having to take care of his invalid brother during the Nazi occupation. One of the Gestapo officers had taken Bruno under his wing when he discovered Schulz's talent for drawing. In exchange for protection he hired Schulz to sketch fanciful fairy-tale figures on the walls of his young son's bedroom: races at Whitsuntide, harvest corn spirits, Easter bonfires—things like that. I guess this was a common practice among German officers, who would keep certain Jews as lackeys if they proved to be useful in some capacity: a tacit code of the "Master Race." Competitive jealousies soon arose among the Germans about who kept the best Jew in tow. Bruno was shot through the head with a Luger by a rival officer while carrying a loaf of bread back to his helpless brother.

I ordered a short stack of buckwheat flapjacks with extra wild blueberries, a side of bacon, and black coffee. I turned to the chapter called "Father's Last Escape," where Bruno describes his dead dad as having metamorphosed into a scorpion.

"A new age began—empty, sober, and joyless, like a sheet of white paper." (Schulz, after his sister had been lost at sea on a voyage to America.)

Blackmail Dialogue #2

"Should I pretend that I don't even know you?"

"How do you mean?"

"Like I'm a stranger—just sitting there waiting?"

"Waiting for what?"

"Waiting for my life to begin?"

"Don't get—"

"What?"

"Don't get esoteric and fancy."

"Fancy?"

"Like you know more than you do."

"I don't."

"Let's keep it simple. It's just a meeting."

"About what?"

"These conversations—these recordings of yours."

"You don't believe me, do you?"

"I want to see them."

"To verify they took place?"

"I know they took place. I just want to see which ones you chose."

"I chose the best."

"The best?"

"The best of the best."

"Nothing's that good."

"How good?"

"Good enough for a book."

"They don't all have to be like punch lines."

"I don't mean that."

"I think it would be exciting if we pretended we didn't know each other."

"Impossible."

"Well—as best we could."

"Impossible."

"Don't keep saying that. You don't know until you've tried."

"How do you 'try' to not recognize someone? Once you've recognized someone, it never leaves you. The hair—the contours of the face—mannerisms. It's all instantly implanted."

"Maybe you can unlearn certain things."

"Like what?"

"Maybe—suddenly—it all looks new and different."

"How so? How could someone's mannerisms look different?"

"Maybe they've had a stroke or an accident of some kind."

"An accident?"

"A car accident."

"No—the underlying person would remain the same."

"What if they've had plastic surgery?"

"Plastic surgery?"

"All bandaged up."

"Like *The Man with the X-ray Eyes*?"

"Who's that?"

"Ray Milland."

"Who's that?"

"Never mind. Just a physical change in a person is not enough to believe it's a completely different person than the one you know."

"Why not?"

"Say, it's simply aging. You haven't seen someone for a very long time. Their teeth are all gone. Their hair. They're all bent over. They walk with a limp. They shake. They can't speak."

"They're all fucked up."

"You still know who it is. It might take you a while, but you still know who it is, don't you?"

Other States

Outside, in Manny's wide sunny parking lot, groups of middle-aged women from other places, other states like Indiana or Iowa, are donning brightly colored rocket-shaped bicycle helmets with perfectly manicured flashing nails, adjusting toe clamps on their pedals, guzzling vitamin water from chartreuse plastic bottles. Everything sparkling and shiny. Older men, who seem to be outfitted in various versions of early Santa Fe caricatures—trappers, vaqueros, Comanche shamans, herbalistas, etc.—squeeze themselves into Porsche roadsters and Audi sports cars, adjusting wraparound shades and checking their gray, greasy sideburns in the rearview mirrors.

I head down the gravel apron off the Old Taos Trail, where vendors are hawking everything from chainsaw sculptures to crow replicas fashioned from rusty barbed wire. A man who owns cedar firewood stacked neatly in the bed of his truck wants a hundred dollars for the load. He's cut all the wood himself. We start grabbing the split logs and throwing them by the armful into the bed of my pickup. The cold air smells of fresh cedar and pine. The Sangre de Cristos. We work in silence. He wears heavy mule-skin gloves stained with oil and gasoline. A sweat-marked hoodie hides his face. I wonder if he's silently cursing me in Spanish just for being a gringo. Our labored exhales cross paths above the red-veined wood.

Dogs are both gone when I get back. Should've never left them roaming like that. Usually, after a good hard chase, they just hang around by the house panting, but this time they're gone. I take the pickup around the motley neighborhood, whistling for hours with my load of cedar clunking in the back. I creep along at a burglar's pace with the windows rolled down so they can hear me.

It's a shrill whistle. I start to feel it's maybe me, alone—my whistle coming back—whistling for myself. It could be that. Wouldn't that be weird? Pathetic. I hear it coming back, each time a little weaker through repetition. Cold, too—ungodly cold. Jaw and lips are freezing. Numb. I pull over, roll the windows up, crank the heater to eighty-five. Hot air blasts my face straight on. Can't find the in-between of hot and cold on the ragged dials. While I'm fumbling, I look out to Los Alamos in the distant Jemez range, engine idling, patches of snow gleaming between the junipers.

I see two men in an office of the White House; one tall and elegant with a dark fedora and a cheroot—the other short, common, and balding, in a three-piece suit. It's some time after '45. Maybe it is '45. The bomb-bay doors of the *Enola Gay* have already opened and Little Boy has been silently released, never to be called back. The Nuclear Age comes to life in a blinding band of white light. My father and all his brothers, in full khaki uniforms, surround my Iroquois grandmother. It's their last chance for a group photo. Beaming smiles—the heroics in the air fill all their hearts with buoyant American pride. Only my grandmother reveals a slightly melancholic twist to her lips. In the background, there's an apple tree in full white bloom.

The man in the fedora is pacing, smoking his cheroot, confessing to the little bald man sitting at the desk; a portrait hangs above him of Jefferson with the ancient future brightly ahead. The tall man is fully confident that the little bald man will coalesce and understand his moral plight. He's telling him he has "sin" on his hands, that he's known "sin" firsthand. His lips are moving. I can see them. I can tell at this distance that it's the word "sin" he's using by the ignominious grin on his face. A Jewish New Yorker, raised in a school of ethics, married to a communist, dabbled in Buddhism, and here he's using the word "sin," plain as day. I can see it! The little man's face turns crimson as he rises slowly up out of his plush leather seat. He calls the tall man a "pansy" and kicks him unceremoniously out of his office, with orders never to return.

Now, a rumble goes through me. My father is flying at midnight under the Nazi radar in a gigantic B-17—the infamous Flying Fortress. His copilot sits beside him, stony-faced. A technician, belly gunner, and bombardier complete the crew. They're all from the same little town of McHenry, where their fathers are busy raising winter wheat as big around as your thumb. They all wear the same leather jackets with the same fur collars turned up. Tiny replicas of bombs are cut into the sleeves with razors and stained red with iodine. Each little bomb represents a mission safely accomplished. There are eight rows of little red bombs. The B-17 maintains a suicidally low profile over Hitler's Romanian oil fields. It's pitch-black night. They begin blanket-bombing acres of fuel. Monster orange flames spring up behind them.

I continue my search for the dogs, prowling through frozen back roads, past miserable ribby horses standing barefoot, hooves split on ice. My whistle is coming out like a faltering teakettle now.

The Reason I've Come Back

The Blackmail Girl was just sitting there. In the living room. Sitting on the edge of the leather couch. Legs tightly together. Back straight. Hands folded neatly in her lap, like a country girl waiting for a bus to the city. In fact, she was so still and poised I'd walked right past her several times without even knowing. That pacing you do when thoughts take over and the body's abandoned to its own devices, its own nervous boredom. You don't even know it's your own house you're walking through. When I first saw her and stopped like someone not sure of what they're seeing—I said nothing. She spoke first. She spoke without looking at me. She was either looking down at her shoes or the floor in between. I forget which.

"I want to talk to you," she started. "The reason I've come back is because I want to ask you some things. I don't want to scare you. I don't want to scare you at all. What I want to know—well, first of all, first of all, the obvious."

"The obvious, what?"

"The obvious is that you're attracted to me. Isn't that right? Now, whether that's simply because I'm so much younger than you—or whether it's because I'm young and female—or—"

"Young and female—yes. That's it—both—and smart."

"Smart?"

"Well—not dull."

"Not dull. No. Never. But what was all this—"

"What?"

"This—drunkenness—this—this—show of bravado."

"Show of bravado? What?"

"This bragging of suicide."

"It wasn't bragging! You don't brag about suicide. There's nothing to brag about—"

"Then what was it?"

"I thought you simply might be interested."

"In what?"

"The way two people, romantically inclined, might agree to—"

"Romantically inclined?"

"Yes."

"But we're not—"

"No—them. *They* were. Not us. The victims."

"What victims?"

"We've never even taken our clothes off together. You've never even seen me naked."

"No!"

"Never kissed. Never touched."

"No! Well—"

"That once—"

"Yes."

"But that was by accident."

"You wanted to see my—"

"I did not!"

"Well, let's not get distracted by—"

"It's simply not true!"

"The point is—"

"What's the point?"

"The point is—"

There was a pretense toward searching for the "point." As though it might be flying around in the air, buzzing, and we were both waiting for it to land. Chunks of last night's fire still glowed in the black corners of the fireplace.

"The point is, I guess, that there's never going to be a sexual culmination to this. Is there?" she said.

"This, what?"

"Whatever you want to call it. And if there was—if there were it would probably be disappointing to us both."

"Disappointing? In what way?"

"Not in that way. I don't mean—"

"What?"

"Sexually. I don't mean sexually."

"You mean sexually disappointing."

"No. It wouldn't be, I don't suppose."

"No."

"Why don't we try it then?"

"No!" She stood fast and walked to the window overlooking dead cactus and an old bocce court with yellow weeds crowding the corners. She held her face in both hands. There was no going to her, touching her—trying to console—like some married person.

"I came back in order to ask you something."

"All right—"

"Do you think it might be possible—"

"To what?"

"To just have an—exchange?"

"Isn't that what we're having?"

"I don't mean—"

"What?"

"I mean—ideas."

"Sure—"

"I mean ideas that mean something. That lead somewhere."

"Where?"

"I don't know—" By this time her hands were down at her sides and then she crossed her arms on her chest and looked out the same window at nothing. It wasn't that there was nothing out there. It was that her look was devoid of seeing. It also wasn't that she was seeing inwardly, it was that she was not seeing at all. A kind of blindness with her eyes wide open.

"Don't you miss your wife?" she said abruptly. The question blindsided me, for sure. She was glad to get it off her chest, I guess, although she didn't turn around to see my face. It took me a while. I sat on the leather couch where she'd already made a dark, warm pocket in the leather and I stared at one of the fading chunks of ember.

"Of course I do."

"You never talk about her."

"No. What's there to talk about?"

"I mean—what happened? All those years and then suddenly—"

"What about—what about this idea of yours—this exchange you're talking about."

"What about it?"

"Well—what's it mean? What do you have in mind?"

"It occurred to me that there must be this swimming of ideas between people. This sea, if you will. Ideas known and unknown. Both. Moving in and out of each other. Feeding off each other. The two of us. Fields, so to speak. Symbiosis, maybe."

"So what?"

"They must be related."

"Why?"

"They're all human. The mind—space—imagination—you know."

"You're making this up."

She turned to me. She looked shocked.

"You look shocked."

"I am shocked—shocked that you might think I'm lying."

"Not lying. I didn't say lying. I said 'making stuff up.'"

"Stuff?"

"Things. Ideas. 'Swimming ideas.'"

"I'm not!"

"You may not know it. I'm sure you don't."

"Know what?"

"The fabrications. Yourself. The weavings of your own imagination."

"Oh!" She shouted the "oh" as though the insult of it were beyond her comprehension. She turned away from me again and the urge to run came strong and she had to catch herself and hold her ground. She wasn't sure anymore what she was doing. Why she'd come back. What this whole thing was about. All "theme" seemed to have run dry.

"I don't know what I'm doing here."

"I don't know what you're doing here either."

"I thought I knew."

"You convinced yourself that you and I had something in common."

"Don't we?"

"What happened? Your friend drove you to the airport and then you had him turn around and return sixty-five miles? That makes a hundred-ten all together round trip. You went a hundred and ten miles out of your way just to come back and—what did he say? Did he ask why you'd changed your mind or if you'd had a change of heart or—what was going through *his* mind? What was going through yours?"

"I was determined to get to the bottom of this."

"This what?"

"Whatever it is—whatever it is that drew us together. I was not going to run away from it."

"Is that what it was? The 'aunt in San Francisco'—running away. Is that what it was?"

"No!" she shouted, and turned her back on me again. Silence boomed.

"Look," I said after a lot of time had elapsed. "Look—I don't know what I'm doing here either. Things just happened— exploded. Now I'm seeing things."

"Seeing things?"

"Yes, my father, for instance. I see my father in everything. He just pops up. In miniature sometimes. I see him in my walk—my whistle. I see him flying planes. Bombing villages. Fires far below. For no good reason."

"Fires?" she said, as though the word left ash in her eyes.

"Isn't it incredible, though—that we could both be in the same exact predicament and not know it?"

"You mean, not know it collectively, or—"

"Just—not know it."

"What else do you see?"

"Things. Animals. Gargoyles, I guess. Slimy things."

"Demons?"

"Sitting on my chest in the morning."

"Oh my God."

"Staring at me."

"You're in worse shape than I thought."

"You can use my guest room again if you want it. I mean, you can continue to use it. I haven't washed the towels."

"I might stay the night."

"What else are you going to do?"

She didn't answer. I left the room. I couldn't stand it. I listened for her movement, but there was none. Right then I wished I was still smoking. I would have had one or two. I stared at plastic medicine bottles on the stone counter of my bathroom. Heart stuff. Vitamins. Inhalers. Aftershave. Razors. I heard small leaves blow up against the screen in the window, clattering, as though they were talking. A neighbor, far off, calling to his son. She came in behind me and started running the bath. That was the first thing she did. Out of nowhere. The hot tap, full blast. She leaned across the porcelain and grabbed the box of epsom salts, as though she'd done all this before. She poured at least half the contents into the steaming water. She set the box down and began to softly talk to me as she took her clothes off. I could see all this in the medicine cabinet mirror, as though I had eyes in the back of my head.

"I made up my mind to come back right after I'd dropped the keys in the return box. I parked the Honda and dropped the keys and then hiked out to the highway again. I never even called my friend."

"So you must've hitchhiked then, or hiked on your own little feet."

"Both. I got one short ride with a Mexican hauling some wood."

"Were you rehearsing the things you would say to me?"

She wore no bra. She had those kind of adolescent breasts with tight, erect nipples and hardly any cup to the breast itself. She slid off her black panties and tested the water. She was completely shaved down there except for one little tuft of black fur. I watched her slowly submerge: hands gripping the edge, mouth agape. Her lips never moved. She sat on the dissolving mound of epsom salts, mashing it down. No sound came out of her. She leaned her head way back against the tub and then sank entirely, eyes closed. Her hands slowly came together over her pussy and the hot water kept gushing, making its deep gurgle. I left before she had a chance to come back up to the surface and open her eyes. I went out to try the dogs again. Now that my lips had warmed up maybe my whistle would be improved.

Maybe she's actually onto something. Something I've missed altogether. Something between the lines, fallen between the cracks. Maybe there's an untold story being told in spite of us. In which case I should step aside in deference? And give her complete "authorship," if that's what she wants. Is that what she wants? Who knows? If I missed it—if I missed it, that's something altogether different. That's just plain "not seeing," that's what that is. These "conversations," as she calls them— exchanges of ideas—thoughts—whatever—are just the groundwork for a whole tapestry of experience. My exchanges with hers, hers with mine, are, in fact, ways of investigation. How could I miss the most glaring truth? If that's the way it actually was. If that's the way it is then so be it, as they say in the King James Bible. "So be it." If, however, it was just a way of "coming on" to her, attracting her attention, getting her interested in "me" and not so much in what I was talking about—what was I talking about? It had to do, as I remember, with her position on the edge of breakaway technology and mine, which was simply a twentieth-century infatuation with empirical existence. Both of us were talking out of our heads, at least I was. Getting nowhere fast, is what my uncle used to say. The remarkable thing is that she would have thought there was some value in it. I thought we were just getting to know each other. That's all it was. Was it something more?

BERLIN, November, 1811

"They repaired to the Inn at Wilhelmstadt, between Berlin and Potsdam, on the border of the Sacred Lake. For one night and one day they were preparing themselves for death, by putting up prayers, singing, drinking a number of bottles of wine and rum, and last of all by taking about sixteen cups of coffee . . . . This done, they repaired to the banks of the Sacred Lake, where they sat down opposite each other. Heinrich von Kleist took a loaded pistol and shot Madame Henriette Vogel through the heart, who fell back dead; he then re-loaded the pistol and shot himself through the head."

Henriette Vogel

I wonder what Henriette Vogel really looked like? That's the first thought that hit me. Terminally ill with uterine cancer, she was not the first woman von Kleist asked to die with him, but she was the first to say yes. Was she cute? Curls? Black lace-up boots. Stacks of starched petticoats.

My whistle comes back. Sailing out over the juniper. I go crunching into frozen chaparral. I wonder if the "farewell letters" were saved? Each of them, Henriette and Heinrich, sitting across from each other in the creamy candlelight, writing with a goose quill. Would they have passed the letters back and forth? Passed the quill? How do you say good-bye to someone forever when they're sitting right across from you? How do you write from the dead when you're still alive? How did he get her to agree, is what I want to know. Of course, she was dying already, but—how was she so sure he'd blow his own brains out after she did the same to hers? Why wasn't there a simultaneity contract of some kind? Both of them poised with pistols at their own temple or both of them poised with the pistols aimed at each other's. What was to keep him from wiping his hands of the whole mess? Just standing bolt upright after he'd shot her and marching off to do some more living. After all, he was only thirty-four. Plenty of juice left. Why wouldn't he have second thoughts once he felt her warm blood splatter across his face when he pulled the trigger? Once he saw her skull explode from the impact? Once he realized this event was now really taking place and that it was not just an idea; a philosophical point of view, a political act of thumbing one's nose at society; just another perpetual rumination. How, indeed, did he talk her into it? Surely, it couldn't have come on the first date. Maybe the idea only slowly occurred to him or maybe even the idea was hers. Maybe she wanted to die worse than he did. Maybe it's what attracted them to each other in the first place. They were made for each other. It was fate.

Sticky Rugs

He's standing now. Wobbly. Moving in a slight zigzag toward the dark bathroom. He wonders if he'll make it. Wonders if he'll make it all the way, or if they'll find him in a heap on the Mexican tile. Lately, there've been spasms, clenchings at the calves and feet—strange little electric jolts around the neck. Could be nothing. What do they call it? "Functional pain"—that's it. "Functional." Means nothing. "Don't turn any lights on, you know the way. You know this house. This one." There was a morning when he mistook it for one of those motel rooms off Highway 40 West, outside Little Rock. One of those little rooms where you sleep in all your clothes because the sheets are slightly suspect. The rugs are sticky so you keep your thick blue socks on. Yellow neon somehow breaks through the paisley wallpaper. Faded prints of the *Mayflower* muscling gigantic Atlantic waves. A laminated desk that's never been sat at with attention. Pocketknife graffiti. Traces of cheap wine spillage or vomit—can't be sure. Stains. (These signs can often be misleading.) He props his hand against the rippled simulated adobe wall above the toilet and takes a leak. He lets it just run out of him slowly, leaning slightly forward, looking down into the water swirling in a clockwise vortex. His piss stinks for some reason. A high, rank vegetable smell like spoiled carrots.

You'd think, not drinking, that wouldn't be the case, but it is. Definite stink. Maybe the asparagus last night. Asparagus and pears. Could be. He shuffles in his blue thermal socks back out of the bathroom, down the hallway, into the kitchen, and turns both dogs out. Big, wiry dogs. Ugly, if you look at them in bad light. They charge out the door, growling and slipping on ice, crashing into each other like hockey players, and disappear into the dark junipers. They're onto something. Something unseen. Maybe the morning light from another time. Coursing whippets, lurchers—jackrabbits plunging out of wet thickets of marsh grass. Traffic in a low hum, far off—echoed through waterways preserved for mallards, white egrets, and sandhill cranes.

His family lies asleep. All of them in different positions. Dreaming. It's still dark and foggy enough that the orange globes of light from the Golden Gate are glowing strong. Enough to believe that this time might live forever. The whole wide bay curls menacingly in its silent cross-currents. Just waiting. He's a boy no longer.

Piebald

Dogs are running with the cattle. Weaving in and out. Noses close to the ground, stuck on a scent. Little random fires in open range. A very small colt—piebald with blue eyes—has picked me up in town and followed me out here. He came running over like he knew me. I'm very skinny, sunburned, bare feet, maybe thirteen. I'm stretching a T-shirt over my bony ribs. This little colt (he's not a pony) is like a dog in his signs of affection. He looks right in my face with a mute query. Can't tell if he's hungry or not. It doesn't seem to be food he's after. He's in good enough flesh. He's light fawn with jagged white patches, like a pinto. Blistering hot already and the sun is barely up. Suddenly, there are people all around. They all seem full of energy and purpose—single-minded. They're onto something. The girls all know me like I'm their brother. They're all moving from fire to fire with bundles of clothing, as though packing for travel. Nobody's sad. Nobody's lamenting. (I usually get unaccountably sad when I pack.) Everyone's young—under thirty. There's no music. No talk. A tacit agreement I seem to be let out of. The surrounding hills are bleak and everything looks like middle South Dakota, out near Kadoka. No threat surrounds us. We're on our own. Black cattle dot the landscape and keep moving through smoke, in and out of the fires. None of the calves are bawling. No fence. No wire. We're all moving somewhere together. I feel as strong as I'll ever be.

Strange Fans

What I can really remember is this: the old man, methodically picking the shrapnel scars at the back of his neck. A mesmerized glaze to his eyes. Far off. Perhaps the past. Perhaps the war. Perhaps. Him, with a tin cup of black coffee, standing in the middle of an avocado grove. The coffee steaming in the morning light. Irrigation. Smudge pots. Strange fans. Him, at breakfast with a hunk of toilet paper plastered to his chin where he'd cut himself shaving. A red dot weeping through. Him, silently reading García Lorca in Spanish. Cervantes. Lips slightly moving. Again. A trance. Him, playing his own kit of drums—drums he'd found in a pawn shop. Drums he'd created. Slingerland bass, stripped of its varnish. Him, playing Wilbur de Paris over and over on a vinyl 78. His pipes in a Bakelite circular holder, white teeth marks bit into all the black mouthpieces. Cartons of Old Golds. Six-pack of Hamm's. Him, warming up the Kaiser-Frazer as though about to take off on reconnaissance.

It was the fifties—Eisenhower was building his highways. America was on a flashing new street. Electric! The Great War was over now. Men were coming home. Women all had their arms wide open.

Opposite Felicity

The thing about Felicity was how opposite she appeared to be in her pure white cotton dress and tan legs, black patent leather pumps and purse to match, how opposite to her naked screaming self I'd remembered that other morning, tossing her red hair. Abandonment. Now, here she was in a ponytail just standing, very straightforward, on our front porch with her arms crossed quaintly, purse dangling, asking if my father was home. I told her he was still at work at the feedlot but she could come in anyway and wait if she liked. So she did and I got more and more nervous and shaky as she sat on the edge of a straight-backed wicker chair while I got iced tea from the cooler and poured it in a Mason jar and brought it to her with the broken ice rattling around and the tea sloshing over the edge. (This was a different house than the boardinghouse. Way out in the country, but Felicity had found it somehow, tracked us down.) When I gave her the tea she put her little black purse on the floor and perched the Mason jar on her knees, then smiled at me with sudden elation.

I got so nervous I had to go outside and walk around for a while. The whole time I was out there I kept imagining her sitting in the wicker chair, all alone with the iced tea balanced on her knees and looking around at our strange new house—

new, I mean, to us—different—different things on the wall
that didn't belong to us, cheap prints of muskellunge and log-
ging camps and places that had nothing to do with the place
in which we now found ourselves. I missed the black rotating fan in our kitchen while I wound my way through patches
of bullthorns, side-stepping old bean cans. The friendliness
of its counterclockwise rotation. The sun was really beating
down by then and I kept seeing it all in my head: the little fan
blowing wind on the back of Felicity's neck, wisps of red hair
standing straight out. I imagined her just sitting there with
her back straight to me and the Mason jar shedding water
down her legs, evaporation running in cold streams down her
calves. I thought maybe what I should do is get up closer to the
house and take a peek through the back window and see if she
was still sitting there or if she'd maybe stood up and strolled
around through the rooms (there were only three), trying to
see if she recognized any of our stuff from the boardinghouse
like Dad's shaving bowl or my chipped accordion. When I got
up close like that to the window I felt like a spy or someone
sneaking around someone else's house and peeking in to see if
there was anything worth stealing. A Peeping Tom. I couldn't
see Felicity at all. The wicker chair was empty. The little black
fan was rotating and blowing air through the empty room. I
could almost feel the rushes of wind. I snuck around to the
bedroom window and saw her bouncing up and down on my
dad's mattress, plunked flat on the floor. There were no sheets
or covers on it, and its dark coffee stains were in sharp contrast
to Felicity's dress. She seemed happy—silently laughing, holding one arm straight up over her head, dripping the Mason jar,

tea spilling out over her shoulders and onto the bare mattress. She turned the jar over completely and poured the tea all over her head. She kicked off her black pumps and jumped up and down, then threw the Mason jar at the wall. It didn't break, just bounced off the sheetrock and rattled around in the corner. Spinning. She stopped laughing. She stopped jumping and just stood there, staring at the wall. The Mason jar twirled to a standstill. She didn't move. I didn't either. She had no idea I was staring at the back of her wet head.

Mother Knows Best

Don't you understand? I don't see why you don't understand. You behave like that and you expect everything to be normal? With him, I mean. How can you do things like that? You go and buy makeup and you behave like that. Right in front of him. What do you expect?

Lanterns

I asked Felicity once about my dad. She was there again, waiting for him. Sitting in the wicker chair with her little black purse and her dust-coated pumps. This time in a frilly pink skirt. (I guess, to look more innocent.)

I asked her if she ever actually talked to him, and she told me he was mostly the silent type. That was one of the things she liked about him, his silence. "Did he *ever* talk? Or just move his lips?" I asked her. "Once," she said. "He talked about disappearing— how everything was disappearing. How there used to be bonfires everywhere, people running with torches. Laughing. The night was full of sparks. Songs. Little children running and screaming with glee. People in love would jump across the snapping flames, hand in hand. Fires would shoot straight up to the stars." "When was this?" I asked her. "The old days, he told me. Back in the old days, before electricity was pulled out of the earth, I suppose. Lanterns lit the unpaved roads."

Something about her voice hypnotized me, even at that age. Something like a hand softly stroking the top of my head. I'd seen horses put to sleep that way by barely rubbing their eyes, their lashes. That's how it's done. I thought, What if my father knew what I was thinking? What was going on? What if he knew I had these feelings about her? I didn't even know what they were yet. These feelings. They felt like warm water running down my back.

Swollen Eye

She is standing now in a white satin dress that clings to her body. She wears nothing underneath. This dress has a pearl-white, almost bluish sheen to it. Shimmering. Luminescent. It falls to the ground and gathers around her feet like a Greek statue. Her body is young. Her face isn't and never looks directly at me. She seems not to recognize me at all, although I know I've been around her for years. Her right eye is swollen red and wide open. It's about three times the size of the other one. I'm standing opposite her in green boxer shorts, holding many soiled towels tightly to my chest in a bundle. I'm asking her where the laundry room is but she doesn't seem to know. She seems lost and doesn't understand why I would be asking this mundane question. She stands there rotating her head from side to side, scanning the space mechanically. As her head swings, the swollen eye passes and peers intensely, trying desperately to recognize me but failing each time.

Wind is kicking up over the mountains now. Sangre de Cristos. Styrofoam cups, dust, and jagged pieces of metal flying across the highway. The junipers and chamisa stand stoic but blowing around the edges as though ready to take off any second. Astroturf putting green has no clue about the coming wind. Little numbers on sticks of steel leading down to white plastic cups. People are going to church in this weather, holding on to their hats, helping the elderly out of cars, protecting their babies from the sun. "Please, dear Jesus, let this not last forever."

Blackmail Girl Rumination

It could be that her intentions were entirely different when she started out. She simply wanted to make note of my inflections—where I put the accent—she had no ideas of plagiarism at all. Listening to the "voice," she discovered the essence. She might have discovered something the speaker was unaware of, in which case she could viably call herself the "author"—the one who knows something more than the speaker himself. The one who tracks something through contrast and disharmony. The one who discovers the undiscovered writer underneath. Maybe that's it. She thinks she knows something about me that I myself don't know. She knows me better than I know myself. That's possible. It's very possible that she might have heard something. A rhyming cadence of some kind. Greek or—Mongolian—or something altogether foreign and unlikely. She became excited about it. It was her little secret. Welsh, maybe. Maybe Welsh. In any case, she felt she made this little discovery entirely on her own, and therefore she was entitled to some kind of authorship. Some kind of something.

I had decided to track her the best I could. I followed her into coffee shops, birdseed stores, pharmacies. There had to be some way I could bring charges against her but I wasn't ready, I realized, to account for my own position in all of this. In fact, I wasn't sure what my position was. I'd like to think of myself as totally innocent—a victim of circumstance—but quickly realized I'd be seen in another light because of our extreme age difference, hers and mine. I mean, it appeared obvious, the lasciviousness, the leering. Besides, she hadn't really done anything yet—she hadn't published anything or proclaimed herself to be "the author" of something she wasn't. She'd just sit for hours, sipping her coffee, staring at her screen and occasionally running her fingers rapidly across the keys, making that cracking, clicking sound. She'd sometimes sit at bus stops with both hands crossed on her laptop, waiting for something to happen—at least that's what it appeared to be. Maybe that was the whole thing—waiting for something to happen, as though her life were in a holding pattern, just waiting for the right moment to land.

Blackmail Dialogue #3

(Little Jerks)

"Why won't you come and see me? I didn't mean for this to be the beginning of the end for us—"

"The beginning of the end of what?"

"Whatever it is."

"It's nothing."

"Don't you believe in accident?"

"Accident is nothing to believe in. It's just something that happens."

"Random."

"Yes."

"Chance."

"Look—"

"What?"

"If I agree to see you—"

"Then you would? You'd consider it?"

"Yes—but don't bring the pages."

"Why not?"

"I don't want to see them."

"Why not?"

"I just don't."

"But you'd like to see me?"

"I'd like to see if you've lost your mind or not."

"How could you tell by just looking at me?"

"Your movements."

"What about them?"

"If they lacked spontaneity or not."

"Spontaneity?"

"Yes."

"What does a lack of spontaneity look like?"

"Jerky."

"Jerky?"

"Yes. When you change your mind, you jerk."

"All of us?"

"All of us."

"I didn't know that."

"Watch. Next time you change your mind."

"And you'd see that in me if we met up?"

"Absolutely."

"How?"

"Your head. Little jerks."

"Side to side?"

"And up and down. Both."

"Little jerks?"

"As though a mosquito were in your ear."

"And how is that indicative of insanity?"

"The mosquito doesn't exist."

Seen Me Seeing Her

I wander a little farther from the house, whistling and calling. The blood rushes out of my hands from the cold. I blow on my fingers and shove both hands deep into the pockets of my jacket. I start seeing her naked, in my head. This might be naive but was she actually trying to seduce me? Was the whole procedure well thought out and full of intent? She couldn't have just suddenly, randomly decided to take a soak in my tub with me standing right there, watching. She must've seen me seeing her in the cabinet mirror. She knew what she was doing. There was a strange lack of titillation to the whole thing, though. A week ago I could have almost died to see her naked, but now—I don't even remember getting a hard-on. I would've remembered that, wouldn't I? I'd certainly remember that. Maybe it was something altogether different.

The dogs are back. Slinking at the front door, panting and meekly wagging their tails. Could be they've been back all this time, lurking around the house, and I just hadn't noticed. There's a lot I don't notice these days. I let them into the kitchen, glad to see them although secretly wanting to kick them both in the ribs. They drink together at the rubber bucket, lapping and dripping. I pull cactus spines out of their pads, then open cans of horrible-smelling coagulated chicken guts. I can smell, along with the guts, the steaming water laced with epsom salts drift down the hallway. I wonder if she's fallen asleep in there. I can't hear any splashing or lapping. I start mixing the chicken with kibble into bowls and the horrible stink recedes somewhat. It suddenly strikes me that she could be in there bleeding to death. I swallow the nervous shock that runs through my throat to my chest. I stop mixing dog food for a second and just listen to space. Dogs panting and wagging. Blue jays squawking. Don't go running in there, whatever you do. The water will be red. Her head will be near the surface. Her eyes wide open. Both her hollow arms will be floating and bluish. The arteries of her wrists slashed. With what? She brought something. A razor. She found one of mine on the bathroom counter. Streams of red will still be swirling, surrounding her waist. Her hair streaming out behind. Her purple toenails protruding. Red fingerprints, clutching at porcelain. The washrag floating squarely between her feet. What will I tell her parents? I just found her that way. There was no indication—who do you call first? The police? No! Not the police. The emergency squad? SWAT team. Who is that? What hospital? Hospital? She's already dead. How do I explain her state of mind? What was her state of mind? Where did we meet? How long ago? Did we ever have sex? What was she doing in my house? In my tub. Totally nude. The body bag. Following the ambulance. No flashing lights. She's already dead. She's already gone.

I slide the aluminum bowls toward both dogs and head down the hallway. I take my time. I see traces of her along the way. Notebooks. Pencils. Textbooks. Computer. Stuff lying around. A silver bracelet. A brass ring. I try to assume an indifferent self. Calm. Unpresuming. I push the bathroom door all the way open. It bounces back slightly. I stop. Don't look down at the tub. There's water all over the floor in puddles. Her clothes are gone. Even her sandals. What was she doing wearing sandals in winter? Don't look at the tub, I keep telling myself. I do. She's gone. Tub's still full. Water's gone lukewarm. I pull the chain on the white plug. The sucking sound seems delayed. Water starts to funnel toward the drain. There's one thin string of blood dancing in the middle. Red and yellow, part of it transparent. A ribbon. Maybe she started something and quit. Thought better of it. No, that's way too rational. She was already in a state. Wasn't she? Didn't she say she had come back to ask me something? Something about an exchange. Why had she been sitting so still for so long? I assume it was long. Waiting. Not moving.

I follow the wet steps of her exit. Has she got a towel? Is she drying her hair, carrying her clothes on her arm, her sandals dangling from two fingers? Two. She couldn't be bleeding. No sign of that. No spots. No smears. I follow her into the guest room. This must be where she finally gets dry, gets dressed. Gets changed into something warmer. All the clothes she took off are lying on the bed. Her sandals too. I check the closet. On the floor her huge suitcase vomits clothes in every direction. Underwear. Panty hose. Patent leather belts. Sweaters. Socks. Her blue parka is gone. The gooseneck lamp on the table beside the bed is still on. Yellow notebooks scattered. I pick up one, scrawled in blue ink: "ARE YOU CRAZY? YOU COULD BE SET FOR LIFE—ALL YOU HAVE TO DO IS

SAY YES!" Another pad reads: "SYNESTHESIA. MUST BE. WHAT ELSE? COLORS? D-MINOR IS DEEP BLUE." I cross back out of the guest room. The side doors leading to the rock patio are wide open. The dogs are already out, heads to the ground, switching their noses to her scent. They both knew her. Went with her on her regular morning jogs. They follow her steps. How could she have walked almost right past me? Where's she headed? By now it's getting colder.

———

It's so cold. Something in his body refuses to get up. Something in the lower back. He stares at the walls. Is there something that might draw him up to at least a sitting position? Listening? The rustle of something? A small creature on the prowl in the rafters. The idea of a fire in the kitchen hearth. Dogs stirring. Coffee—at least that. The appendages don't seem connected to the motor—whatever that is—driving this thing. They won't take direction—won't be dictated to—the arms, legs, feet, hands. Nothing moves. Nothing even wants to. The brain isn't sending signals. That's it. Signals. No sign of danger, even.

Blackmail Girl on the Loose

I went looking for her. I did. I'd had enough of being alone. I wanted her with me. She knew that. She got excited about it in her voice, but it didn't bring her any nearer. I kept returning to the little corner café where we'd first met. Isn't it always like that? You return to the place, hoping she'll miraculously show up, even though she might be miles from there. Maybe the other side of the moon. I kept ordering the exact same thing I'd had on the morning I first met her—two eggs over medium, with corned beef hash, no potatoes, and a toasted English muffin. As though, magically, the same order would call her back. The waitress was the same, "Betty." Dyed red hair with blond roots showing. Tattoos of roses and barbed wire on both forearms. Her complexion seemed oddly brown and not just from sunlight. She remembered me but not the Girl. I asked her. She studied the picture window as though the Girl might appear outside, in a parking lot puddle. "Nope. Don't remember that one. More coffee?"

"Yes, please." Betty walked away, scribbling on a green check pad. The Girl had questioned me thoroughly about my past—my teenage years. Examining me as though I might be correct for her future, as though I might measure up to some standard she had. I told her I only remembered passionate necking with dark Mexican chicks. Girls in tight skirts with black eyes and Indian noses. Pink lipstick. A constant hard-on. Even after coming. The smell of it would follow me, wherever I went. Dogs knew.

My dogs knew. I felt certain that adults could smell it too. Especially white middle-aged women. The way they'd look at me and smile, then look down at their open-toed heels. I loved older women. Their hips. Their leather purses with the straps. Their wide-brimmed hats. I'd follow them sometimes in grocery stores. The ice cream section where cold steam came pouring off the frozen boxes.

"I want to talk to you," she kept repeating. "I want to ask you something." As though she'd never really gotten a chance. As though I were always distracted. Maybe I was. Why are you here? Why are you always coming back?

"Do you have some idealized notion in your head of the way things might be between us? I mean, do you see ideas pouring off each other night and day, mixing like some giant Cuisinart machine coming out in genius mixes of chocolate and gold?" I said.

"Chocolate and gold? What're you talking about?"

"Exactly."

"You're making no sense."

"No."

"Do you remember Oklahoma? The two of us?"

"Oklahoma?"

"Yes."

"Were we there?"

"Just the two of us. Nothing around but the occasional oil

jack pumping away like a miniature cartoon dinosaur. We walked for miles without saying a word."

"We were talking about synesthesia."

"No. I remember miles of silence."

"D-minor was seen as aquamarine. Middle C was orange."

"We discussed this?"

"You're too young to be forgetting."

"I remember something about colors."

"Sound?"

"Sound and colors. Yes."

"Synesthesia?"

"If you say so."

"I do."

We walked and walked and found ourselves down by this riverbed. There'd been a drought that summer so half the river was dried up. Also, local oilmen had been stealing water rights and selling them to Big Business for fracking purposes. Dust and cracked ground with the sun beating down and then, suddenly, there'd be one little stretch of water trickling into a pool where the bed was a little deeper, then back to baked earth. There were huge boulders down there, right in the middle. At one time, frogs and turtles would bask in the sun then flop back into the river when danger approached. Now these boulders were just sitting there numbly, cooking in the sun as though sent down from deep space, crashing and forever embedded. We walked out there and climbed them. They were hot to the touch. We lay down side by side on one of the big dark flat ones. We stared up at the gap the canyon walls made and the clouds moved across it, leaving a long strip of blue. I looked up through the flicking poplar leaves and remembered a shot from a Russian "art film" back in the sixties where the camera started gratuitously swirling in circles. It made me sick to my stomach. The stone was so warm it felt like the body of a huge animal beneath us. Maybe a mastodon. Asleep there forever.

I remember she said she hated the wind. Any wind that was constant. She remembered all the different names for it. Different countries: the "mistrals" of France, the "clippers" of the Alberta plains, the "dust devils" of the Sonora, the "chinooks." There was something about the wind that drove her crazy. You could see it come over her. Eyes. Her mouth hung open. Even her hair took on a different color.

Someone Else's Life

One other morning when Felicity came by with her same little black purse and sat on the same wicker chair, waiting for my dad, who was always at work, I got up the courage to ask her why her face always looked so blank. She told me she didn't know what expression to use because she didn't understand other people. I asked her why not and she said that she always had this feeling of living someone else's life and that people seemed way outside her somehow. Apart. I asked her who the other person might be, the one living her life for her, and she explained that she didn't know how but it was someone her same age and female but she didn't know her name. I asked her if she knew what lay up ahead: if she had some idea what her future might hold. She told me, no, it wasn't like that—"Like what?" I asked. It wasn't as though she could see the future. It wasn't as though things were laid out and all she had to do was go through with them. It was as though her experiences didn't belong to her. They belonged to someone else.

I sat there a long time in silence, staring at the floor. Felicity was good at silence. Better than me. She seemed to have no anxiety about what lay up ahead. She could take it or leave it. My fear of her mounted until I leaped up from the couch and tried to make up some excuse to go outside. She didn't seem the least bit nervous. Nothing had changed in her. She just kept sitting on the wicker chair in the same way she had before, with the patent leather purse in her lap. I ran outside onto the back porch and started tossing all the pails of warm slimy dog water out and refilling them. Just for something to do.

Far-Off Banging Doors

The violence of these dogs. The barking as though life and death were on the line. And the woman who says nothing. She's deaf. Whether she partially hears the dogs doesn't matter. She says nothing. They could sound to her like far-off banging doors. It doesn't matter, she says nothing. Just walks up and down a long hallway with short arthritic steps. Scarves flow from her neck. She has bright blue cowboy boots. She speaks lovingly to plumbers, electricians, people up the hill who are responsible for flooding her basement, insurance companies, she doesn't care. She has mean scars all over her body. Knife wounds. She ignores them. She's deaf. I have to spell out the restaurant we're going to. We're going to eat outside. The weather is perfect. One lone cricket is making his little sound.

Tiny Man in an Irish Pub

Night: They're playing darts in an Irish pub. You can see them through the glazed window, leaning toward the target. Three of them this time, still dressed up in their pinstriped suits, fedora hats, and those shoes you always see them wearing in black-and-white movies—pointed—brogans, I guess. With little indented holes or perforations in the pattern. They're all smoking Luckies and drinking martinis with green olives and a twist of lemon rind. The '49 Merc is parked outside with a fourth guy propped against the trunk, his foot on the bumper, dressed exactly like the others. He's smoking and shuffling a deck of cards, separating the one-eyed jacks. None of these characters look like actors but they all seem to be playing a role.

Inside, the other three are laughing and chewing on toothpicks as one of them throws his set of darts at the wall. Each time he throws he leans in, squints his eyes, and makes three little practice strokes with his right arm before releasing. My tiny dead father, still wrapped in Saran, and two of the shrunken women are hung on the target by the necks with pink rubber bands. They bob up and down ever so slightly as the darts zoom past their heads. One dart with red feathers and a golden streamlined point hits my father square in the forehead and sticks. The tiny body spins. He's already dead so he doesn't make a peep. The gangsters are hysterical with laughter as they take sips of their drinks and adjust the bold knots of their ties.

Two more darts are thrown at my father, who is still spinning. They both miss. One grazes his shoulder and clatters to the floor. One guy makes a yellow mark on a chalkboard. The third guy drops a dime in a Wurlitzer. This is about all I can remember.

Blackmail Girl Monologue

It's me again. Only to remind you that your days are numbered. You've been found out. I guess you know that by now. I guess you don't need me to remind you. It's just the satisfaction I get at seeing you squirm. In my mind's eye, as they say. Of course, there still is a way out for you—an avenue of escape. You can reconsider altogether. You can hand over the authorship to me entirely. You won't be blamed for anything—any falsehood—lies—distortions of any kind. You will be left blameless. Entirely blameless. It was never your fault that you stretched certain "truths." That you doctored certain events in order to give them "poetic justice." That you jumbled others in order to give them a new impression of meaning and ongoingness. That you're just as confused as you always were. You might ask me why I would be willing to take on such a deceit and I would tell you, plain and simple, that it's my pleasure to join up with the old world. Avant-garde, if you will. The twentieth-century werewolves of forgotten lore. The ones who saved us from corporate nihilism. The ones who walk the mini malls, head down, fingering Molotov cocktails in their overcoat pockets and occasionally blowing themselves up. Just like the old days. Just like the good old days of yore.

———

I remember one time having a conversation with Felicity about the past. The past in general, as though we were suddenly in the throes of philosophy. It was, again, one of those times when she'd ostensibly come by to see my father and my father was, of course, not there. One of those times she was, again, sitting on the wicker chair with the tea balanced on her naked knees and her purse on the floor beside her. She told me she thought the past was the present. That was her idea: just like that. The past was the present. She just came out with it. With a straight face. It wasn't every day we shared ideas like that, but evidently this was something she thought about all the time. She told me this moment we're in right now that we call the "present" is actually becoming the "past" and we don't even know it. "That means we're all living in the future because we're witnessing the present become the 'past,' as we speak." I didn't know what to say. I made up some excuse to go into another room.

Across the Desert Floor

I told her she had to go. I didn't know why. Just came out with it. I made things up. You should've seen the shock on her face. Her incredulous green eyes. I told her I couldn't stand her dog shedding black hair everywhere. (I made that up.) I told her I couldn't stand her own wiry black hair with the white roots everywhere. In the sink. In the bathtub. In the shower. In the toilet. On the sheets, the kitchen counter. (I made all that up.) I really didn't know why I wanted her gone.

She cried all the way down to the airport. Seventy miles across the desert floor. She had on a linen forties vintage dress that clung to her skin. Her legs were exquisite. Her hair was pulled tightly back into a ponytail, which gave her face a rictus of grief. Water poured down her neck. Something in me separated her pain from her attractiveness. I tried to rub the back of my hand down her smooth thigh, but she rejected me.

When we arrived at the boutique hotel on the desert floor, we had lunch. She checked into room 506. I tipped the valet guy five bucks. There was a Mexican wedding going on in the lobby. Women with frilly purple-laced petticoats and bougainvilleas in their bouncy hair. The men wore tuxedos and polished boots with pointy toes. They took lots of photographs with an old-fashioned Kodak flash attachment that lit everything up and made you feel blind for a second. She was accidentally in the background of every shot while she and the dog waited for the elevator. Still crying. Weeping. No one knew.

After lunch (watermelon salad and artichoke hearts), we went up to the tiny room on the fifth floor. She broke down again, once we got up there, and told me she couldn't stand to stay in there all night long waiting for the plane the next day. I said that's why I had asked her if she was sure she wanted to drive all the way across the desert floor to the hotel rather than wait at my place in the mountains overnight. She told me she hadn't realized it was going to be so horrible.

We left all the baggage there and kept the room. I tipped the valet guy again, for nothing, just because I was nervous, I guess. He seemed suspicious of us.

We drove all the seventy miles back, across the desert floor to my place in the mountains, where we'd just come from. We drove in silence for a long while. Once, I asked her if her ears had popped and she told me they had. I repeated that I just needed a little rest, that I felt a need to be completely alone in order to write (but that was a lie too, because plenty of times before I'd been able to write in the midst of a roomful of people, back when I was nineteen or twenty).

We passed Bernalillo, where my father was killed, and I remembered a great café called the Range where you could still get green chili and eggs, but we'd eaten already. It was almost time for supper by the time we got back so we ordered paella to take out from a Spanish tapas place. Paella and a Diet Coke for her (I was already into the silver Tesoro by then). She decided to make a peach cobbler out of peaches that were going bad. I went into town to get the food. On the way back a bobcat sauntered across the road and disappeared into blackness.

We had to push all my writing to one end of the table to make room for the food. The grayish-blue Olympia typewriter (my pride and joy) went in the kitchen on the granite countertop. She got suddenly happy when she tasted the Diet Coke and smiled at me across the table in that most beautiful way she has. She told me she liked having dinner alone with me at the house. Just the two of us. She used the word "romantic" a lot. I told her I was going outside to light a fire.

She had, just the day before, established a link system of some kind in order to receive wi-fi. Now she could have ready access to all sorts of movies. (We were way out in the rural haunts.) After dinner she got undressed and pored through hundreds of movie ads on her laptop. She sat cross-legged on the bed with the computer casting a bright band of light across her exotic face. Her dog lay sound asleep on a horse blanket with the King Ranch brand woven into it. I was outside all this time trying to light a fire in the wind.

The wind was kicking up in every direction. My stick matches kept blowing out until one finally caught the edge of a brown grocery bag with the words "I'm Local" printed on it. The coyotes were howling in high-pitched screams, as though the wind were tormenting some nerve in their ears. The dogs joined in from the kitchen. I let them out and they went straight after unseen rabbits.

Much later, in the dark, I staggered into the bedroom, where she was still undecided about what to watch. Lots of movies came up on her screen: *The 400 Blows, La Notte, The Magnificent Seven, Chitty Chitty Bang Bang.* Movies I saw in high school. I watched the ads go by, calling up times that I must have coasted through. Times that I barely remember being there for. I don't remember what I was doing, who I was with. Inside myself maybe. Or outside. I told her I wouldn't mind seeing the documentary on the Roosevelts. They always fascinated me as a kind of American royalty. Something plebeian and yet down-to-earth about them. Down-to-earth—what an expression. The narration for the Roosevelts had a condescending tone, but the still photographs in black-and-white were interesting. Amazing how the camera captures time without even trying.

Next morning I woke and sat straight up. I could feel her breathing beside me. It was completely black. The wind was still blowing slightly. The metal shutters clanged on the wooden window frame. When it got light we drove the seventy miles back across the desert floor to the boutique hotel again. She was dressed the same. I had the same physical reaction but I didn't try to touch her leg. Her hair was pulled back in the same severe way. She looked straight ahead, out the window. There was something hieroglyphic about her. Regal.

At the hotel I tipped the valet guy again and told him to come upstairs to 506, get the luggage, and then throw it in the back of the Chevy. He seemed more suspicious than before, but accepted the tip. I went and ordered us some room service breakfast while she took the dog up to the room and put the luggage out in the hallway. We had about an hour before we had to check in at the airport. We ate the omelet with red peppers and goat cheese—me sitting on the AC unit while she sat on the very edge of the bed with her legs crossed at the knees. One leg bouncing rhythmically, marking time. She stared out the fifth-story window while chewing slowly, the fork poised below her chin. She spoke almost in a whisper: "What a horrible little town. What do people do?" I said nothing. There was a tinted photograph on the wall of a fifty-year-old man dancing a Cuban rumba with a ten-year-old girl. She was dressed all in white. He had her bent backward from the waist and was holding her like he would a full-grown woman. "You'll never get rid of me, you know." She spoke without looking at me as she cut another mouthful of omelet with her fork. "I know your reputation for discarding women, but you'll never get rid of me."

We made love like a couple who hadn't seen each other for quite some time. Not like two people who were saying good-bye, perhaps forever. Not like two people who couldn't get along and had decided to call it quits. She screamed so violently I thought maybe the valet guy might hear her down on street level and grow even more suspicious when we reappeared for the car.

We got dressed. I got the leash on the dog while she brushed her hair and put fresh gloss on her lips. We went down to the lobby. I got change for a twenty to tip the valet guy yet again. He looked at me funny when I gave him the tip. I was right. I knew I was right.

We arrived at the departure entrance for United, and my heart was pounding for some reason. I gave her some money to get a luggage cart. There was a long line of them, all strung together like you see at the Safeway. We hugged and kissed as I loaded the luggage on the cart. There were no tears. No hysterics. Her dog got suddenly excited and started leaping all over her. There were no tears at all.

I drove back the seventy miles across the desert floor, alone. I was glad to be alone. I had no thoughts one way or the other. No remorse. The sky was full of airy white clouds. The sky, powder blue behind them.

I went straight to the house. I wanted to believe I'd done the right thing. I'd asked her to go so I could be entirely alone to do my work. I washed some clothes that were lying on the floor. I put fresh birdseed in all the feeders. I chopped kindling. I pruned fruit trees. I transplanted plants. I made iced tea. I washed dishes. I made the bed. I couldn't get to work on my writing. Nothing was stopping me, but I couldn't get to work. I called my oldest friend in El Paso—no answer. I called my ex-wife in New Orleans—no answer. I called my first wife in LA—no answer. I called my long-lasting girlfriend in New York—no answer.

I woke up at 3 a.m. Ink black. The wind had stopped. The dogs were asleep in the kitchen. I felt there was somebody else there with me. I listened.

Diné Kid

The bright, bright southwestern sun splashing all the white cars in the parking lot. The hoods doubly hot with internal combustion and solar heat. A Denny's on the very edge of Grants, New Mexico, squashed between 40 West and some Shell. Dry weeds, black plastic stuck to them, trying to blow free. Shabby chain link surrounding all this. What chance does beauty have to sneak in?

I'm in some side booth behind a frail man with his chubby wife, his back to me. A straw Western hat folded in the Sonoran style (taco side fenders). Deep track marks above his cheekbones say he uses oxygen all night. Just over his shoulder I see her at a distance. Just the back of someone. Voluptuous—curvaceous—looks to be about thirty but when she turns slightly sideways it's more like forty. Tight white pedal pushers and leather sandals. T-shirt with a Harley skull. She's covered from forehead to toe in tiny, purple tattoos—more like totems than machine-made designs. Small swallows, hawks, lizards, and moons in all phases. She turns and her face is much older than I thought—at least forty-five, maybe more. But her body's so young. She has a boy with her. A crippled Indian kid with an aluminum walker. Heavyset. Maybe twenty-two. Butch haircut. Glasses. His eyes never leave her as she helps him into the booth, parks the walker outside, and takes him by one tortured arm. Gets him to sit, then slides in beside him closely. He smiles at her. There's nowhere else in the world he'd rather be. She opens the colorful Plasticene menu and stares at photos in color of waffles and eggs and whipped cream. He never takes his eyes off her although his crooked hands open his own menu. He lies across the table. Both arms limply out in front of him. Useless. Helpless. He cradles his head in one elbow and smiles up at her. She continues to study waffles and pancakes. "I want to move in with you," he says. She smiles but keeps studying the menu. "I want to move all my stuff in with you and sleep in the same bed. Can I?" he says. She smiles and reaches out with one hand. She places it softly on his butch haircut and strokes his head with her long green fingernails, just like you'd put a horse to sleep. Her eyes never leave the menu. Her eyes close. She rests her head on his shoulder.

Son of a Just Man

"So, when you left me—"

    "I never left you."

"Okay, when you went away—heading west."

"I never left you."

"Don't be dramatic."

"I want to be clear."

"What are you, a lawyer now? Clarity? Language? When you drove down to Nashville to visit that woman with the big ass, then continued on Highway 40 toward Little Rock, Fort Smith, Oklahoma City in that perpetual daze of not-knowing, in that hapless state of being led by the cock—"

"What about it?"

"Did you ever once think of why it was you might have happened to ask me to marry you?"

"No."

"No."

"No, I didn't."

"Did you think your asking me to marry you might have caused me to think about the future? About domestic bliss. About front lawns and bedroom linens?"

"No."

"About rings and bells and barbecues with the relatives?"

"No."

"No, of course not."

"I didn't."

"Did she get herself waxed for you?"

"Who?"

"The woman with the big ass from Nashville! Did she get one of those Brazilian jobs or did she leave a little strip of fuzz?"

"A little strip of fuzz?"

(*Long pause here as he slowly turns his head and stares out at the dreary, overcast day that reminds him of Donegal, in the north of Ireland. The soft, light rain descends at a slant and coats the naked peach trees with a milky film.*)

"What would you be doing right now if you were alone?"

"Right now?"

"Yes. If I wasn't here."

"Pretty much the same thing as I'm doing right now when you *are* here."

"Nothing would change?"

"I don't know—a certain 'state of mind,' I guess. What's the matter?"

"You would be thinking about something else, maybe?"

"No. *Feeling. Feeling* something else."

"What would you be feeling?"

"I wouldn't be so concerned about you. Your presence. Distracted by your presence, I mean—"

"You're concerned about me?"

"Well, you know—you're on my mind all the time. You're—always moving around—one room to another. Ideas must cross your mind. Ideas about me. Silent ideas. You must think—"

"What?"

"You must think: 'This is not my home. It's his home. He lives here but not me. I am a visitor. A visitor in his life.'"

"How does that change the way you feel?"

"It just does."

"How?"

"I don't really want to talk about this."

"Why?"

"I just don't. It makes me tense in the chest. In the throat."

"Why?"

"You sound like a kid, a little child. 'Why? Why? Why?' all the time."

"I'm interested. What would change if you were alone?"

"I just told you."

"You didn't. You told me nothing."

"I told you—I just don't know how to explain it. Something would change. That's all I can say. Some—feeling. Some—sense of things. Some—"

"What?"

"I don't know! I guess there would be an absence—a missing. Something incomplete."

"Really?"

"Yes, I think so."

"I feel incomplete all the time. I don't know if it's a person I miss or—"

"What?"

"A time. People from the past."

"Dead and gone?"

"Some?"

"People you never knew?"

"Maybe."

"Maybe your parents?"

"No, they're alive."

"You don't miss them, then?"

"Not in that way."

"What way?"

"Like you'll never see them again. Gone for good."

"Yeah, I guess. You don't need them, then?"

"Yours are dead, aren't they?"

"Yes. They're dead."

"So all you have are memories. Photographs."

"There's this one where my mother must be around eight or nine and it's late summer. Alder trees are in leaf behind her. Gooseberries are full of fruit. She's wearing a little white lace dress with a big scalloped collar, knee-length socks, patent leather Mary Janes with straps at the ankle, and a knit cap with her bangs pushing through. Her head is cocked to one side with a tiny smile that looks as though she's embarrassed about being photographed—about being witnessed. She's standing in a gravel driveway next to my great-grandfather, Frederick DeForrest Bynon. 'Bynon' means 'son of a just man' in ancient Welsh, which is what he is, a Welshman. Frederick is the father of my mother's mother, Amy. He is very tall and distinguished with a full white beard and mustache, dark three-piece suit, a pair of wire bifocals hang on a chain from his neck over a high-collared dress shirt. His left arm dangles a flat-crowned straw hat by the brim and his shoes are freshly polished. It could very well be a Sunday 'go to church' day. Who knows if they're going or coming? At the top of the photograph in faded longhand it reads 'Dunbar—August 1, 1921.' And at the bottom in the same hand, 'Grandpa and Jane Elaine in Driveway.'"

Heading North to Shiprock

I guess I was lucky to be alive back then, when you get right down to it, purring along on Baseline Drive in Ed Cartwright's '40 Ford with a Mercury flathead and the Stones full blast on KFWB—Color Radio Channel 98—and Anita Guttierre in the back seat with her skirt around her neck and bottles of Ripple and bags full of bennies and the hot summer winds blasting shafts of orange blossoms through the windows. Nothing wrong with that. The unknown is sometimes better. Sometimes way better. Don't you think?

Felicity Close Up

One image of Felicity I'll never forget was of her singing when she was about eight or nine years old. It was a foreign national anthem in some language I'd never heard. She kept forgetting the words to it. There was a huge audience like for a World Cup game in a giant coliseum but you never saw them. All you saw was Felicity close up in a parochial school uniform of some kind with suspenders and a white blouse. Her head was tucked into the belly of a middle-aged man in slacks, white shirt, and an alligator belt. It must have been her father but you never saw his face. Just his hand, now and then, stroking the top of her head very affectionately. Very soft. A blue jeweled ring gleamed from his index finger. It had two crossed tennis rackets etched into it. Felicity was singing the foreign national anthem to the huge audience over a loudspeaker system but she would grow unbearably shy and silent, then try to disappear into her father's pocket. It was as though she wanted to become a tiny mouse and hide inside the dark folds with his car keys and loose change. She kept looking up at his face for relief but you never saw his face, just her, looking up, almost pleading. She never cried but you could see she wanted to be somewhere else, anywhere but there.

Maybe it's like that. A foot. Hand. Or idea. Something slips. Shifts. You find yourself in another world. You weren't even looking. It just arrived. Appeared. Like a deer at dusk. Sudden. Still. An ear twitches. Another ear. You're not alone. You don't even see it. It sees you. Maybe it's just like that.

Wafer-Thin Paper

She called me from the road, said she was heading north in a rented Jeep and she'd spend the night in Chattanooga at a Hampton Inn—her favorite, I don't know why. She'd already done six-hundred-some miles and was dog-tired. It was raining buckets here but not there, apparently, although I didn't think it was a good idea for her to drive at night. Funny, I immediately became concerned about her, alone on the road at night, as though we were still living together after all those years. A couple with parts of each other somehow embedded. Parts of each.

She arrived and unloaded her stuff—cameras, a leather portfolio, her photographs and the dark archival boxes that held them in bows and ribbons with her name carefully engraved on the front. The way she ran her hands over the contours of the pictures and the wafer-thin paper—the white tissue that separated each photo—I thought this to be very female in the best sense of the word. She made it known right away that we would be sleeping together in the convertible couch and not her stuck away alone in the upstairs bedroom like some houseguest. I had no argument with that. We went out and had dinner at Henry's place—crowded as always but we found a good booth. My temptation to have a glass of red wine was overcome by how glad I was to see her. Henry was his usual very courtly, very gentlemanly self. There was horse racing on the little television over the bar, broadcast all the way from Florida. I didn't even know that Tampa Bay still existed, actually. The restaurant was full of "racehorse" people—trainers, jockeys, and the very wealthy who owned acres and acres of bluegrass and white mansions with Greek columns and fields of tobacco and soybeans and corn.

At night we settled in with books on the North Pole and Graham Greene novels. I tried to get her to read some short stories by Bolaño but she found them too depressing and pejorative in a strictly male sense. We talked about our children when they were very young. How our little girl was always making our little boy laugh. How he tried to keep a straight face but she kept cracking him up. We talked about how remarkable it was for two stubborn, crusty, old codgers like ourselves to have spawned such mild-mannered calm kids. I tried killing a bluebottle fly with an empty laundry bag and finally succeeded. The whole time I was thinking of this French woman who wrote an entire essay about the death of a fly. The outright tragedy of it. Suzuki with a whole blank page of his book *Beginner's Mind* devoted to a picture of a fly. No words, just a fly. Alive.

We became addicted to the TV series *Breaking Bad*. We bought a forty-inch Samsung TV and a DVD player at Target just to play the series. We bought ten episodes and started our watching from the pilot, right on through. Neither of us had ever seen the series or watched a show in this manner, in sequence. Just black blanks where the commercials were sup-

posed to go. The two kids who were working at Target seemed suspicious of us when we each admitted we knew nothing about technology and we had no idea what plugged into what. They claimed it was simple. They should have seen us unpacking the stuff back on the farm.

We sat on the porch in the pouring rain and talked about an island off Alabama that opened out to the Gulf. I immediately had fantasies of ocean wind. I could hear sea gulls, and brass fittings banging in the bay. I could smell fish and eel. She told me it was all in my mind. Palm trees waved.

We took a long walk up the driveway when the sun came out and I pointed out the tall white oaks and the hickory with thorny little nuts already protruding. She stopped at every clump of new mushrooms in caps of yellow, pink, and gold. The Elkhorn was running muddy and fast, far below.

Later that afternoon, she fell asleep on the leather couch as I read *Mornings in Mexico* out loud by D. H. Lawrence. Later she read me something by James Agee. Something about old men on a front porch at dusk.

She told me exactly what was going to happen, as though the future were already past. She told me that as soon as she left the farm, I would call "that young porn star" and bring her down here. She said I would continue to lie about other women and I would continue to have all these "affairs." I denied it. I denied all of it. I opened the farm gate for her. She rolled down the window. We kissed in the afternoon shade. She drove away. I closed the gate.

Dirt Back Road

"Would you rather be alone? Just tell me."

"Right now, you mean?"

"Yeah. Right now."

"Instead of being with you?"

"That's what I mean."

"Well, if I said yes, that would be an open invitation to an insult, wouldn't it?"

"To me, you mean?"

"Yes. To you."

"You would have to run the risk of hurting my feelings."

"I would like to imagine that I wouldn't think about the risk."

"Then you'd probably hurt my feelings even more."

"Why is that?"

"Something callous about it."

"Callous?"

"You would stop being my friend."

"Are we friends now?"

"I thought we were."

"You're not sure?"

"Well, I know we've been through something together. Lived through something."

"What?"

"Experiences. Time."

"Riding around in the car?"

"Looking out the window."

"Commenting on certain things we see out the window?"

"Eating breakfast."

"Coffee."

"Five-grain toast."

"Sleeping in the same bed."

"Fucking."

"Well, yes—fucking."

"Coming together."

"Sometimes."

"Sometimes you, sometimes me."

"Watching me get dressed up for you?"

"Is that what you were doing? All that time?"

"Didn't you know that?"

"I was wondering why you watched me like that."

"Now you know."

"All that time."

"Going out to dinner."

"Yes. All those things."

"Are those things you'd rather do alone?"

"Me?"

"Yes. You."

"No, I was asking about *you*. Would *you* rather be alone?"

(LONG PAUSE)

"Do you think about me when I'm not here?"

"You?"

"Yes, do you picture me? Do you imagine me alone somewhere? Daydreaming. Fantasizing. All by myself."

"About what?"

"Anything. Being somewhere else, for instance."

"Where?"

A very small diner on a dirt back road. Night. No cars. Very few lights. A lone dog in the distance. A metal table with a white tablecloth. A candle made out of beeswax. One other couple. Drunk. Very drunk. Loud. Talking about baseball. We try to get away from them without being noticed. We try to get some peace, politely. They follow us. They sit down at the table right behind us. They continue to talk loud about baseball and the World Series. They get louder and louder. Especially the woman. They're from somewhere else. Colorado. Utah. They know they annoy us. They want to annoy us. They seem to enjoy the agitation they're causing. We both get up from the table. You go off to find the waiter in the kitchen, in order to pay him. The woman starts to insult me. The man laughs very loudly. The woman makes fun of the way I'm dressed. My hair. The shoes I have on. The man laughs even louder. I walk off in the direction I saw you go to find the waiter. The woman follows me, weaving. She grabs hold of my long braid and won't let go. I whirl around and hit her square in the face with my leather handbag. I knock her to the ground. The man starts yelling at me. The woman is so drunk she can't get up. She starts crying and screaming and clawing at her ankles. The man takes hold of my shoulder and jerks me around. You come out of the kitchen, having paid the waiter, and knee the man in the nuts. He screams and falls over the short railing into the dirt road. The lone dog barks louder in the distance. The woman starts yelling frantically for the police, who are nowhere to be seen. The man crawls pathetically around in the dirt like a wounded crab, clutching his balls, groaning and coughing, shouting lewd insinuations at the night sky, which is lavishly spangled with stars. The little waiter comes out of the kitchen wiping his hands on a dirty towel and chewing on something brittle. The two of us head for our blue beat-up pickup truck parked across the road. We walk calmly, arm in arm, like a couple entering the Copacabana. The man yells from the floor of the dirt street that he's going to kill us both. He's going to find out where we live. The exact address. He knows people who are in the know. He's going to let us rot in our bed. He's going to murder us as we're copulating. He's going to wait until we've almost reached the point of ejaculation and then he'll pull the trigger. Right then. Right in the moment when we've both come together in perfect syncopation and feel as though we're one ecstatic luminous being ascending to the heavens. Right then, he pulls the trigger.

A Girl I Know

There's no guarantee against these nightmares now. I just
let them come. Every morning at almost exactly 4:22.
Black. I've left one window open just to let the cool night air
pass through my room and give the demons a way out. The
demons. The moon is in the window now. There, behind the
blinds—glowing. Grinning. It's gone out of its way to catch
me square in the face. I hear the dogs snoring like old people
from the kitchen. Old people when they fall asleep, teacups
dangling from their index fingers in front of a glowing fire.
This time it's me on a couch high on the cliffs overlooking Los
Angeles. I recognize the place. Early day. An old bungalow-
style complex, with peeling chalky plaster. A girl I know rents
it to me. A girl I know lets me stay in a small room she insists
once belonged to James Dean, before he was famous. This
time I'm outside, stretched out on a red Naugahyde couch,
surrounded by dolly track. Completely encircled. Several
camera operators with their baseball caps turned front to back
(who started that?) race around, their eyes suctioned to the
rubber eyepiece of Rolleiflex cameras. But they're not actually shooting film. I'm the audience, I guess. I watch them
"pretend-shooting" delicately painted cityscapes: murals on
sheets of plywood and canvas. Faded pastels in pinks, blues,

and yellows. Everything subdued. They keep racing from one position to the other, the grips sweating profusely as they push the seated cameraman at top speed. Now and then, they come to sudden stops, zooming in tightly on the murals, then racing on to the next one. The tips of giant eucalyptus sway languidly in the background. Far below, in the valley, you can make out the Santa Monica Freeway, crawling. Up here mockingbirds flit from tree to tree in the growing heat. Suddenly, my couch bursts into flame. A girl I know runs away.

Blackmail Dialogue #4

"Have you given any thought to the cover?"

"What cover?"

"The cover of the book."

"Listen—how far are you going to carry this thing?"

"What thing?"

"This idea that we've somehow or another coauthored a book that contains beautiful ideas. It was simply conversation. Conversation that I thought was totally private and was never intended for public consumption. Conversation that had nothing to with writing."

"It all has to do with writing."

"Oh, here we go—now you've got a philosophy."

"Well, it does. Talking and writing. They're interdependent."

"If you say so."

"I do."

"What do you know about it? You've never written anything."

"Now I have."

"That isn't writing."

"What is it, then?"

"Copying."

"I only wrote down what exists already. That's all I did."

Back Across the Desert Floor

At 2:30 a.m. I started bleeding from the left nostril. I thought I could stop it easily by stuffing my nose full of toilet paper and laying my head back flat on the bed. I stared at the white ceiling fan. No sounds except a lone cricket. When I got up my bare feet stuck to the drops of blood on the brick bathroom floor. When I pulled the toilet paper out of my left nostril, it went right on bleeding. More blood now came out of my right. It was very dark blood and looked like it might have come from some mysterious internal organ. From 2:30 to 5:00 a.m. I thought I could get it stopped. I'd had nosebleeds before. The thing I didn't want to do was to disturb the woman whose guesthouse I was staying in—she had five dogs that really made a racket when aroused. She'd already been kind enough to go my bail and find me a crackerjack DUI lawyer and drive me around town on shortcuts when they'd taken away my driver's license. At 5:00 a.m. I decided to enlist her help. I called both her phone numbers, trying to connect to her main house, but couldn't get through on either. Finally, I decided to walk over there from the guesthouse, in my underwear with toilet paper jammed up both my nostrils and blood splashing everywhere. Sure enough, the dogs went nutty and started howling their heads off. Lila (the woman who owns the house) came to the door in her pajamas and was horrified by the sight of me. She couldn't quite grasp the predicament but understood it was an emergency. We drove to the ER at the hospital in our little New Mexican town, using every back road and slowing for all the speed bumps. (She swore this was a shortcut.) On arrival, someone was waiting with a black wheelchair as I stumbled from the Honda, blood flying. An Irish doctor came and very energetically started packing my left nostril with a cotton material she said was impregnated with cocaine. (It's hard to believe how much stuff will fit up inside your nose.) She was very lively and got the bleeding stopped. The Irish doctor kept telling me that it should be okay now but make sure to have my wife check it periodically and call if anything further happened. I tried to explain that Lila was not my wife, to no avail. We went back on the same shortcut, slowing again for all the speed bumps. My head was propped back with my nostrils packed full of cocaine-gauze, and I kept thinking how nice it would be to be born and raised here and go to prep school here and then on to some fancy Ivy League deal back east and become a lawyer or a doctor and then come back here and have reunions and see your old friends and spend Christmas with your parents who were still alive and give your father plaid ties and your mother turquoise jewelry and your siblings bright red racing skis. We passed the museums on the hill in the early-morning light. Bronze statues of pioneers in various poses of heroic suffering. A beautiful cottonwood tree was the cornerpiece of a soccer field with brand-new plastic netting at both ends for goals. It was too early yet for anyone to be up except garbage men throwing containers at random and jumping back on their truck as though it were a stagecoach. Once back at Lila's house my nose started to bleed again and she got it stopped with a washrag in the kitchen. She called my doctor in Phoenix and he thought I should come down and get checked into the hospital just to make sure. Lila volunteered immediately for the drive and just needed to call someone to take care of the dogs and plants. There was no talking her out of it.

Off we went to Phoenix, across the desert floor, in Lila's Honda with my nose packed and oxygen tanks clanking around in the back seat. We passed Bernalillo, where Coronado had butchered all the locals and my dad had been run over, near the Sage Café—where they serve great green chili and eggs. Albuquerque seemed more boring than ever and it was hard to believe it is now the U.S. capital of MURDER. Probably because there is nothing else to do.

We stopped at the Continental Divide to get gas and there was a sun-bleached covered wagon there with "Elevation— 7360 feet" written on the side of it. We got Subway sandwiches at a Phillips 66 station. Mine was a six-inch BMT with green peppers, onion, mayo, and mustard. I forget what Lila got but it looked green and healthy.

We drove on past ancient meteor craters, Navajo trading posts, dinosaur skeletons, buffalo petting zoos, rattlesnake purses, knife emporiums, concrete tepees, abandoned frontier forts, authentic Zuni bracelets, Apache casinos, adult superstores, Catholic crucifixion stores, agate bookends, Aztec blankets, Elvis Presley T-shirts, Sitting Bull coffee mugs. At Flagstaff we swapped driving and I went on to Phoenix while

Lila focused on her green sandwich. Flagstaff was high and cold. Time we hit the desert floor it was 120 degrees. People were imprisoned by air conditioning. There was tremendous Phoenix traffic, which I guess is now expected in every major metropolis across America at around 5:00 p.m.

We checked into the hospital and they were expecting us. A room overlooking saguaro cacti and heat waves. Many people we passed seemed much worse off than me: bandaged heads, suspended legs and arms, muffled weeping of family members, horrible hacking from the chest, limping down the aisles on aluminum walkers. There was a bevy of nurses at each station—moving in very efficient order with clipboards and thermometers and stethoscopes—all dressed in dark, navy-blue scrubs. Moving like a little army of ants. There were the usual forms and insurance claims to fill out—also living wills, so if you were to suddenly turn into a vegetable they wouldn't keep you going indefinitely on life support. I often wondered what would happen if you were very much alive but looked dead, seemed dead, and were surrounded by the living who also believed you were dead but you had no way or means to communicate you weren't dead. Very much like life as it is right now. A nurse came in and gave elaborate directions, all written down, on how Lila should get to her hotel. Again I had to explain that she wasn't my wife. Again I tried to signal to the outside world that I was marooned, that I had no idea what I was doing, where I was going, who these people were all around me. Again no one listened or pretended they understood when they didn't. When they had no idea. At first they tried very hard to figure out why I was there to begin with. I told them exactly what had happened to me. That I woke up in a pool of my own blood. That I tracked it down to a nosebleed. That the nosebleed wouldn't stop. That I had to awaken my friend Lila (who wasn't my wife). That she took me to the ER in New Mexico and that the next thing I knew I was there in the hospital. They asked me about family. I told them I had none. My parents were dead. My sisters were far away. My children were scattered. I told them I shouldn't even be there, taking up a hospital bed—that there were many others more deserving. They said they understood. They realized there was something wrong with me even if they didn't know how to describe it. I asked them to try. One nurse said that the minute I came into the building she knew. I said, "What?" Knew what? She said there was something about me that was catastrophic. That's the word she used—"catastrophic." She had no idea why I was there, who I was, or where I'd come from. She just knew my condition was "catastrophic" and that I'd always remain that way. "What way?" I asked her. She didn't explain. She was very cute. Diné, or at least half. She had one of those faces that curl up around the edges when she smiled, causing her eyes to squint shut and almost disappear. She wore a hairnet but it never seemed out of place or gave the impression of someone who might work in a delicatessen. She was very athletic and moved with extreme ease. Nothing daunted her somehow. She could accomplish any task. Her name tag said "Anna Tumbo."

That night, after a dinner of meatloaf and mashed potatoes, me and Lila watched *A Fistful of Dollars* by Sergio Leone with Clint Eastwood when he was very young. Early sixties. Terribly, unabashedly corny with the worst soundtrack I've ever heard. The lead woman who was supposed to be Mexican was obviously a green-eyed gringo. The bad brothers were painted so "bad" that you began to like them. Lila sat very still in a gray office chair. She never moved. She never laughed. She never said a word. I lay, propped up, in the bed with an IV. Anna Tumbo came in and took my blood pressure.

Boots with Red Flowers

I told Felicity she had to stop coming around like this—why was she always coming around when she knew my dad was at work? I mean, why was she always coming around? She'd just stare at me and smile. She moved the little black purse on her knees. This time she was wearing cutoff blue jeans and boots with red flowers and pistols carved into them. Very Western. She asked me if there was something against the law about her coming by my place and paying me a visit. She just wanted to see the dogs, anyway. She said. Maybe pick some oranges. Run through the sprinklers. I told her there was nothing against the law, it just seemed weird, that's all. "Weird?" she said. "There's nothing weird about us being friends." She considered us friends. I thought that was great, but at the same time I wondered if that's the way my dad would see it. "Friends"? I mean, what did that mean to her? Did that mean that when I looked at her purse moving around on her knees, that was all I was looking at?

There were times back then when I thought I'd never get out of there alive. I'd have to become a famous golfer or a veterinarian or something like that. I'd have to escape completely. I'd have to take a different name, different haircut, wear clothes from a different era. Start listening to music by

Tommy Dorsey. I don't know. What if Felicity decided to track me down? What if my father found out? What if he decided to do me in or have me arrested or something? What if he went completely crazy? Insanity ran in the family, don't forget. There was some great-great-something—an uncle or a cousin or something—who ran off to live with the Indians back then, had many wives, many children, stopped speaking English altogether, took up astrology, had Cherokee slaves. I don't know. I didn't want to wind up like that, that's for sure. I had to find a way out of there. Completely.

Could it be that I just couldn't see? All those years of hot rods, winning. Tijuana. False ID. Prostitution. Donkey fucking. Breaking the Talc. Race. Sex. Sock hops. Mescal in silver bottles. Tacos. Parking lots. Radios. Benzedrine. Cherry Coke. Brigitte Bardot. Chino state prison. Rock and roll. Hitchhike to Oklahoma City.

I go back, following avenues with the same name, same buildings, but nothing's the same. Nothing's there now but a "community garden." Vegetables. Fruit trees. They must've leveled the whole six floors with a wrecking ball. Little kids watching from rusty fire escapes. Old fat Polish ladies leaning on mops.

Back then it was white chicks with black needles hanging off their skinny bare arms. Sprawled out in the empty bathtub unconscious. A guy at the door in jodhpurs and a riding crop asking for "Benny," as though I'd tell him. His trumpet in a paper sack. Wicker rockers full of junkies. Curly says it's just like Mississippi in here. All that's missing is the slapping screen doors and redbone coonhounds. That's what he tells me. Me—I grew up out west where the eye never stops. All we had for heat was a gas stove. When that ran out we froze. Not that it ever did.

See—she was right here. I'm not kidding. Right here with me in that yellow chair, drinking iced tea. Staring at orioles. Remarking. This place is a virtual crossroads of migration. All kinds of shit flies over. Sandhill cranes, great blue herons, cedar waxwings. You name it. All we have to do is sit and wait. Sip our tea. See—she was right here. Here are her underpants to prove it. Red with white bows. She wore those. Must've left them here on purpose, just to get a rise out of me. I was never sure just what she was after. Maybe nothing. Could be. What was she doing here, anyway?

One particular night, though, one night we had a bottle of red and just parked in front of the fence line where the horses were. She crossed her long legs on the dashboard and we had the radio tuned to some Memphis station—Jerry Lee, Al Perkins, somebody like that. Her blouse was a creamy pink silk and she had on a man's pinstriped jacket with lapels. She always talked with that thick accent of hers from the faraway mountain country where Rousseau used to hide out in that weird getup of his. She'd spit wisps of long blond hair between half sentences, then laugh and sneer like a pirate so that the skin crinkled above her high cheekbones and, at the same time, moisture gathered, mixing with little dots of blue mascara. The headlights made a stripe on the black fence and we could see horses' legs between the lower rails. Above, their eyes gleamed green and yellow, ears twitching, trying to hear the sounds of us humans laughing. At what, I don't know. She found most things silly. Most human things. I remember trying to teach her how to shoot my .410 single-shot. Made in Brazil, of all places. Simple gun. One shell at a time. She couldn't hit a Coke bottle at fifteen feet. She'd blink, close her eyes, and then jump when the gun went off. I told her she'd never hit a thing like that. She just laughed. Drove my Gator straight up the hill with the parking break on—screaming her head off. Mud slung us in the face.

Her idea about America was that it was some kind of playground. A series of disconnected zones that made sense only in the experimental mode. You could go to Los Angeles and live in the midst of a movie—black-and-white or color, made no difference where you were from, whether you were intending to "be" dumb. It made no difference. You really and truly could "blow in the wind." Was it the same in Europe? In that high country she came from where Mozart burst on the scene as a fourteen-year-old, his old man prodding him with a stick. Was it true anywhere else in the world? Weren't American ideas like "education," "trade," "earning a living" still indelibly implanted in the psyche somewhere? Was being born having to be enlisting in a destiny?

Boy Who Fell Asleep in the Shower

He must have changed costumes as least seven times. At least. An osprey flew back and forth across the screened square of window in his trailer. Searing. The black-and-white "one-liner" was folded back to day 42. A breakfast sandwich of scrambled egg, cheese, and bacon lay half-eaten and wet on a crumpled sheet of tinfoil. The coffee had gone cold. They couldn't seem to make up their minds about the sequence. It was a toss-up between scene 68 or scene 77. Random recall crossed his mind. His youngest son, who loved the sensation of sneezing. He remembered. The boy who fell asleep in the shower. He remembered. Curled up naked on white tiles with hot water pelting down. Asleep. His skin turned red by hot water. He remembered that. What was he dreaming?

For scene 68 he wore essentially the same thing he was supposed to wear for scene 77 except the colors were slightly different. This meant changing the entire ensemble. Scene 68 required a raspberry-sherbet-colored linen shirt, khaki pants, alligator belt, blue canvas shoes with no socks and the heels folded in against the insoles, like bedroom slippers. For 77 he was supposed to have on a mango-colored shirt. Navy-blue slacks and coffee-brown tennis shoes with white sweat socks. The alligator belt remained the same. What they seemed to fail to understand was that he, himself, would go unchanged. He would remain always the same.

I get back and she's gone. Back door's wide open. How many times has this happened? Disappearance—empty rooms— fans slowly turning in silence. No note. Sound of a distant leaf blower. The Unspoken—louder than screaming. Her agonized orgasms. Like a slaughtered lamb. Ecstasy was never supposed to be like this. Her deep shudder that goes through the walls and out into tropical trees—iguanas—green parrots—hairless dogs quivering. She told me last night, with a lavender toothbrush hanging from her lips, that her hair had turned completely white at age eleven. Abruptly. Overnight. Just wham like that. Not gray but white. Pure. Not out of fear or despair but white as milk. She immediately went to dying it pitch black. She dyes it now. "Nobody knows," she says. "I'm the only one. And you now." I can see her somewhere running, as a little girl. White hair streaming. As though running away from it. As though her hair's on fire.

I told her I wouldn't be messed with, which now sounds pompous and ridiculous, when you get right down to it.

Now what?? For me? Stuck here in some imitation sugar plantation with hired clean-cut white people running around it in electric golf carts, lime T-shirts with name tags, and pot- ted palms. The pool's so new there's no scum mark where the water laps against the tile. A kid in a flat top and goggles squirts a plastic water gun high above magnolia trees. The spray reaches the deep end. His mother, in a tiger-striped bikini, cautions him that there is now an adult in the pool with him. That's me (the "adult"). I do a crippled version of the Australian crawl and barely accomplish a lap, then prop both elbows in the green drain, panting like a scalded dog. What is this? Adrift. Adrift between lives? Is this the same turquoise sea where we once had ceviche and BBQ shrimp? What happened in between? Where have you gone?

Shrinkage

You seem to be diminishing. Bit by bit. I don't know—
maybe I'm losing my mind. Maybe it is me. Like that guy
when he got back to his super-domestic life in the suburbs
after having encountered a mysterious cloud on the bow of
his yacht. Remember? He checks the notches in his belt. Suddenly, his khaki slacks are several sizes too big. He's swimming
in his shoes. He's shorter than his wife, when he's always been
taller. (This is a movie with absolutely no sense of humor, by
the way.) His wife is extremely sympathetic. She's very straight
with hair like Doris Day. She watches him grow smaller and
smaller. She sets him up in a dollhouse. A dollhouse the man
fashioned for his daughter when he was a normal-sized man.
The daughter's now gone off to college; we never see her. She
has grown up and achieved the size of a normal American
woman and left her dollhouse behind. The man lives his daily
life inside the dollhouse, getting smaller and smaller, day by
day. The wife brings him miniature meals, miniature cups of
tea, she makes him miniature clothing—pajamas, for instance,
and miniature shirts and pants. She tells no one what is happening to her husband. She never sees neighbors or friends.
She gets more and more distressed but keeps it to herself.
(This is the fifties, remember.) She keeps making up excuses

about her husband's whereabouts. The neighbors become suspicious. The man continues to shrink. The woman becomes emotionally shaky.

One day, the family cat attacks the man, taking him for an insect or a tiny rodent of some kind. Something to eat. The wife gives the man a needle to protect himself. She puts the cat in a separate room but the cat gets out and attacks the man again. This time the man uses the needle and stabs the cat in the ass. The cat becomes wary of the man, now knowing he has a stinger. Remember all this? It's important.

Slowly, the man realizes he is going to just disappear. His shrinking is relentless, inexorable. He does not want his wife to continue to suffer responsibility. He sneaks out the back door with the huge needle over his shoulder, barely able to lift it. It's night and the bright porch light reflects the waving blades of grass in the backyard. They look like silver duck tongues. He descends the stairs of the porch using thread from his wife's sewing kit to rappel his way down the sheer vertical face of the steps. He finally enters the lawn, dashing into the cover of the towering blades waving in the night breeze. He keeps running with the needle and thread, colliding into snails, ants, and beetles. Spiders travel noiselessly over the top of him like galactic robots. Owls and bats track his panicked zigzag progress. He's now getting so small that the needle and thread seem to be suspended in their own levitation. Then he simply vanishes. (This is a movie with absolutely no sense of humor.) You must remember this?

You are now traveling. Your future is frozen. Rapidly, you are jettisoned from the blank unknown to the bright clear world. "Day out of days." "Call sheets." Dumped off in front of your white box of a trailer that's been hauled across the country from Burbank for the thousandth time, the name of your character taped on the door in bold black letters. Surrounded suddenly by everyone you've never met before. All of them effusively nice and asking what you might need. Bottled water from Burma? Caramel-coated pretzels? Organic jasmine tea? "Do you have any exotic food allergies?" Captured suddenly in the land of unimagined luxury where everyone seems to know you from a long-dead motion picture forty years ago. How can you begin to explain that you're not that person?

Black Hole

They've rented us a country house for the duration of the shoot in an extremely rural area called Whippoor-will, Oklahoma. (The bird in medieval mythology that was always present as the harbinger of death.) The house is big enough that the Blackmail Girl can have her own room and study upstairs. She's up there now, bent over a thick book called *Chaos and Where It's Going*. I can see her. She might as well be alone. The house is owned by a famous veterinarian who once pampered the hunting falcons of Arabian sheiks. (I should've stuck with animal medicine.) Evidently, this doctor has gone away for a wedding and left us to rent the house. I'm lying on my back, fully clothed, on the veterinarian's king-sized bed, watching dusk slowly fade to night. I'm think-ing about this Girl upstairs, but it does me no good. I might as well be alone. All the accoutrements of falconry hang on the pine-paneled walls, silently awaiting the hunter's return: simulated quail lures intricately woven out of colorful nylon, partridge and duck, shoulder baskets and leather pouches for dead game, bait, walking staves with brass handles in the shape of hawk heads, greyhounds, hoods and blinkers, blind-ers with leather latigo tethers, round stands of synthetic grass for the birds to perch on when they're doing nothing, spiked rods, thick mule-skin gloves and knee-high leggings, antennae and transmitters for tracking lost birds. On the wall above the mahogany headboard is a colored mural of Kublai Khan and his vast, opulent hunting party: four white elephants at the very center of the conflagration, supporting a massive rectangular throne/platform for the warrior chieftain. Green and orange banners stream from every corner of the canopied roof; plush tiger pelts provide shade for the royal party. Fierce mounted battalions of Mongolian hunters, bows and quivers lashed to their backs. Salukis scour the steppes, flushing hare and small rodents. Dromedaries carry leopards in steel cages. Chained cheetahs cringe on the backs of painted ponies. Eagles and owls are tied to green bamboo rods. Sleek peregrines explode into mallards, sending clouds of feathers cascading down on everyone's heads. This is all happening while I daydream. A kind of "day in the life" of Kublai Khan. Some mind invention woven to capture the imagination down through time. As though time were a spiral. As though the ancient past could be conveniently held in your hand. All at once.

The darkening light has now turned the mural to silhouette. I can't hear the Blackmail Girl. Can't hear her turning the pages. The oil jacks have gone silent outside. A lone cow bawls for her calf, but there's no answer. No dog barks. No coyote. Some rustling of small birds in landscape bushes. Leaves tumble. Leaves across cold concrete. A turkey scratches. Gobbles. No frogs. The refrigerator clicks over to a colder setting, down the hall. I can hear her descending the stairs. I can hear her bare feet. I don't move. She appears, just standing at the foot of the bed, materializing out of darkness. Silent. Standing there staring at me with her arms hanging limp. Like a prisoner who's been arrested one too many times. I still don't move. Maybe I've stopped breathing. She's dressed in gray sweat pants, gray hoodie, her hair still wet from the shower. Dripping. She moves to the far side of the bed and stops. I follow her with my eyes. Can't hear her breath. She climbs in under the quilted covers and turns her back to me again, without saying a word.

We fall asleep like that. Silent. For once, I don't dream.

She awoke in exactly the same position she'd fallen asleep in: knees tucked up almost to her chin, hands clasped around them, her back very deliberately turned toward me like a sharply curved little boulder. She stared out the picture window plastered with decals from security companies warning would-be intruders. She stared at the long prairie grass turning pink from encroaching morning light. She knew this wasn't Wisconsin. Even though she wasn't looking directly at me she knew I was awake. I could tell she knew. She began speaking softly without moving, as though to herself and me, at the same time. I stared up at the mural. Colors were shifting. The elephants seemed to be on the move. She spoke in a monotone:

"I had this funny dream about a theme park. Down in Florida, I guess. Just like Disneyland but it wasn't. It was called 'The End of the World' and we were on a ride called 'The Black Hole.' Everybody was screaming and scared. Not us, but everyone else. You couldn't feel anything underneath you. No support—no gravity. The bottom had fallen out. Then we went through this tunnel called 'Apocalypse Now.' I never saw that movie. Did you?"

"Yeah. Brando rubbed his bald head like it was a puppy dog and stared into the campfire. I had the feeling he was proud of the shape of his cranium."

"No one can help how their cranium's shaped."

"True."

"Where were they?"

"It was supposed to be Vietnam but they shot it in Honolulu, I think."

"From a nightmare to a holiday."

"What other rides did you go on in your dream?"

"There was one called 'The Butterfly Effect' where we got separated."

"Did we ever find each other?"

"Yes—in something called 'Complex Games,' where we tried to put ourselves back together."

"What happened?"

"We'd become shattered into all these different pieces. We started handing each other parts of ourselves."

"Very symbolic."

"No, it just seemed like an ordinary event."

"I hate that stuff like *Last Year at Marienbad* and that Bergman flick where he plays chess with the devil."

"I never saw those."

"No, I suppose not."

"You must've grown up in a weird time."

"Wait a minute—who are 'we' supposed to be if we're handing parts of ourselves to each other?"

"I don't know. We're just doing it and getting it all wrong. I mean, my head on your shoulders, for instance. Your feet on my ankles."

"Really fucked up."

"Yeah—"

"Is it supposed to mean something?"

"Just a dream, or a nightmare, I guess."

"What's the difference?"

"What?"

"Between a dream and a nightmare?"

"Fear. Isn't a nightmare full of fear?"

"And not a dream?"

"No, a dream's innocent, isn't it? Light. There's no fear in a dream."

"So when fear enters it becomes a nightmare?"

"That must be it."

"Well, I'm glad we cleared that up."

"Yeah." Still she didn't move. I had an impulse to put my arm around her but I thought it would disturb something. Her train of thought, maybe. Her train of thought chugging down the track. I said something after a long stillness. "Maybe it was the posture you fell asleep in."

"What posture?"

"That one you're in now—knees tucked up—arms wrapped around them." She immediately shifted position. Straightened her legs, pushed her hands deep into her pockets. She kept her back to me. "They say sometimes the position you fall asleep in can have a lot to do with your dreaming."

"You mean whether it's a nightmare or a dream?"

"I guess. Yeah."

"You mean—before you fall asleep—just before—you calculate your posture—you calibrate it, so to speak, for either a nightmare or a dream?"

"Well, I don't know if it would work exactly like that—"

"Who would want to intentionally create a nightmare, anyway?"

"I don't know. Maybe somebody who's bored."

"Are you?" We fell silent again. I wondered if she felt the same remoteness as me at being thrown together in a stranger's house. A stranger's things all around us. People we never met. Everything indicative of a life being lived in this house but nobody's present but us. Pictures framed of grandchildren in crisp clothes, hair neatly parted. A family cat with a scarf for a collar. Closets full of someone's clothes, hanging like dead men from a tree. Plaids and foreign fabrics—things neither of us would ever wear. Shoes way too big. I sat up and swung my legs over, feet flat on the beige wall-to-wall carpet. I came, almost immediately, to a straight-backed position, turning intentionally away from her. She never moved.

"I'm going to see if there's coffee. They must have a coffee maker in the kitchen." I stood.

"I had another dream," she said. "Right alongside the nightmare about the rides in the 'End of the World' park. Right in that same position too. Knees tucked up. Do you want to hear it?" I turned to her but couldn't see her face.

"Sure," I said. "I'll just make some coffee first."

"Your father was in it."

"My father?"

"Yes. He told me he was your father, anyway."

"My father's dead."

"I know that. The dead can still appear in dreams, can't they?"

"He doesn't speak. He doesn't speak anymore."

"He did in this dream."

"What did he say?"

"He wanted to thank you for unwrapping his tiny head."

"He was already dead."

"He wanted to thank you anyway."

"That was nice of him."

"I thought so."

"What did he want to thank me for?"

"For the breath of fresh air. It was the first time he'd felt real air for a long, long time."

"Real air?"

"Air that moved. That came from somewhere else and visited."

"Where? Where did it come from? Did he say?"

"High in the mountains. No people."

"Where?"

"That's all he told me." I stood there a long time. Waiting for something more. I wanted to ask her why he'd become so small but I knew she couldn't tell me. I wanted to ask her where they were taking him and all the others but I knew she couldn't tell me. She never moved an inch.

"I'm going to make some coffee."

Next morning, me and Blackmail Girl appear on the set. Everyone seems befuddled and judgmental now. Even in this era of liberal smugness it causes suspicion—an almost-seventy-year-old man with a twenty-year-old girl. Taboo! Not "age appropriate"! "We don't appreciate your moral perspective." She remains cool—barefoot with a thin silver ring around the next left toe in from the little one. Dark purple nail polish. Heavy blue overcoat that goes clear to her ankles, so no one gets a good look at her body. They don't miss her lavender eye shadow, though, or the wry turn of her lips.

We get inside the trailer and quickly slam the metal door. All the neon bulbs are blaring white. Two of them blink and go out. The thermostat is cranked up to ninety, for good measure. Sure enough, there's a huge wicker basket full to overflowing with dried apricots, pink pears, Emergen-C. Cracker Jacks and a bottle of green salsa. This entire cornucopia nestles on a bed of Easter-yellow straw with a note from a long string of producers welcoming me to the club and wishing me "Bon voyage"—like a new ship about to embark on shining, silky waters with no inkling of possible doom. (Do all actors share an impending terror of this merger into "character"? Or is it just me?)

She grabs a pear and clamps her teeth around it, then drops her long overcoat and sits with her knees propped up. She's entirely naked except for the dark purple polish. She chomps into the pear and says it's too hot for clothes. Juice runs down her neck. She opens the script and studies the yellow-highlighted pages. I start automatically going through my monologues out loud with no attempt at accent or "intention" (I'm not a method actor). She chomps her pear and corrects me each time I stumble.

After she's straightened the collar of my costume and thrown her overcoat back on, we cross over to the makeup trailer. I tell her I want her always by my side, no matter what. She doesn't answer. Keeps her head down, collar up. Mute. Her purple toenails flash through the dead grass. Dusk is moving in. Moisture fills the air. I remember Bruno's question: "What is a spring dusk?" but spring has gone. People all around this movie "location" are living their entire lives behind giant oaks. Tiny lights go on across the fields from hooded porches. I wonder what they make of us? Some glamorous fantasy? Maybe they believe they're stuck and we're the ones who are living the real life. Maybe they believe they'll forever be exiled from a life of their dreams.

Acorns fall in tight clumps. Black squirrels. Pit bulls lash out heedlessly at chain link fence. Security lights pop on in somebody's driveway. Nobody's there.

After makeup we cross back over the dead lawn and enter the set—a clapboard farmhouse probably built in the thirties with a wraparound porch. It's night. Dormer windows smile like little jack-o'-lanterns. Inside, the familiar smell of smoking gels and gaffer's tape sealing the windows tight against any intruding light. The air gets thicker. The chaos of film crews rushing back and forth doing their chores. Pliers, clamps, flashlights, gloves, bounce boards, electrician's tape, apple boxes, booms, earphones, walkie-talkies, high-hats, shutters, electronic clapboards, chalk marks, dolly track. Silent mania. Coded language bounces from wall to wall in hushed urgency. I take Blackmail Girl back to one of the little side rooms and introduce her to the director, who's sitting with the script adviser behind two mounted monitors. I leave her there and go into the set. She can take care of herself.

I'm playing the part of an aging alcoholic who's interviewing an Osage girl for the job of overseeing his pillhead wife, diagnosed with cancer of the womb and needing, of course, to be driven round-trip to Tulsa for her chemotherapy treatments. The actress playing the part of the Osage girl is actually Blackfoot from northern Montana, but who knows Blackfoot from Osage in a mostly white audience at some megaplex theater in the anonymous corporate malls of America? And who cares? An Indian's an Indian. The usual last-minute fussing with lights, props, costumes, hair, is going on fervently while I keep trying to digest the script. It's well written—way better than most— but still difficult to absorb. The language holds the character, for me. Only through the varied repetition of saying words out loud does the character begin to appear like a negative in a chemical bath. The Blackfoot girl seems scared. She sits rigidly on the edge of her chair in her makeup and costume.

I loosen her up a little through simple conversation. Just us two talking in the midst of swirling madness and chaos. I ask her if she knows a friend of mine named Dutch from up there in Browning near her rez, and she does. He's half Irish, half Blackfoot—a stuntman I'd worked with years ago, whose father raised wild-ass bucking horses. They used to drive the whole herd each spring down into Cut Bank to the rodeo arena, right through the center of town. As we're talking, prop masters are trying wedding rings on me, necklaces on her; makeup artists are powdering her face and hands; costume personnel are messing with our clothes; the hair department is combing,

brushing, spraying. Everyone's trying to do their job; we main-
tain eye contact as the business continues all around us, and I
tell her an incident I recall with Dutch where he was doubling
for a "Native American" woman, chasing a white wolf on foot.
It was shot from behind so you couldn't tell it was a man. He
was wearing a long black wig and a double of her costume.
The white wolf had been brought from LA by the peroxide-
blond trainer in a special caged truck a week early so the wolf
could have plenty of time to acclimate. The trainer brought
special water, special meat, special blankets. This was a pampered wolf. Before we attempted to shoot the chase scene,
the trainer gathered everyone together to explain in a hushed
voice the very special conditions of working with a wolf. First
of all, none of us, under any circumstance, was allowed to look
at the wolf directly in its yellow eyes. If we did, then the trainer
couldn't be responsible for the outcome. Secondly, all women
who were menstruating had to be banned from the set—no
exceptions. Thirdly, no loud noises or sudden movements—
if lights were to be suddenly popped on, he, the trainer, must
be informed well in advance. No meat of any kind was to be
eaten at the same time of shooting—hamburgers, hot dogs,
tuna sandwiches, nothing. And lastly, he could only guarantee three takes of chasing, after three the wolf might get wise
to the repetition and turn on the stunt man, or, worse, the
steadicam operator—or, even worse, the whole bunch of us
puny human beings would be torn to shreds. That said, we
proceeded.

Later, as me and the Blackmail Girl head for the huge cater-
ing service tent lit up like a circus tent in the night, she's very

excited by what she's just witnessed on the monitor. I ask her about the scene—if it was at all plausible. "Yes," she says, "but what were you and that Indian girl talking about before the camera was turned on and the scene began?"

"Oh, I forget," I say. "Why?"

"Because I wasn't sure if you were 'acting' or not."

We plod on with the script while I start trying on pieces of costume: vests with gold-threaded embroidery around the pockets, period underwear buttons on the fly (nobody's ever going to see the underwear, but I guess it's a token toward authenticity), high-collared shirts, pearl cuff links. Suddenly I notice—as I'm trying to work the head of a pearl cuff link through the starched slit in the sleeve of the shirt—that the Girl's back is covered in an almost invisible orange fuzz, like a young peach. The neon backlights it. I lick my finger and run it across the tiny hairs just to make sure I'm not seeing things. The hairs stand up. Her shoulders shudder slightly but she makes no sound, just keeps feeding me the lines. The monologues are gratuitously convoluted but interesting to speak—variations, I suppose, on a mannered academic T. S. Eliot voice. An Anglophile poet I was never enamored with—essential ideas redolent of stale gin and suicide. I ask Blackmail Girl to help me with the stiff collar. Little gold studs have to be inserted and attached somehow to make it stand up. She moves to the back of my neck. I can feel her perfect erect nipples brushing the linen of my shirt. I picture them as golden as the little brass studs. I can feel her breath behind me. I know she's there, working away, the script tucked under her shaved armpit. Biting her bottom lip. Intent. Breathing vapor.

Suddenly, the costume team bursts into the trailer hauling shirts on wire hangers over their shoulders. Blackmail Girl doesn't even turn toward them, just keeps working my collar with her tongue hanging out. The team stands there stunned by the nudity. One of them darts back outside. The other one remains stoically and says, "Sorry, I should've knocked."

"That's all right. Just trying things on."

"Does any of it feel like the character to you?" she asks.

"I don't know who the character is yet. I just got here."

"Yes, I know—but, I mean your 'vision' of the character. How you 'see' him."

"I don't have a vision of the character. I don't see him at all. The character. Far as I know he could be a ghost. Someone you hope to encounter in broad daylight."

"I'm sorry," she says softly as she backs out of the trailer, closing the door gently behind her with a metallic click.

Matching Purposes

She had a family, after all. Father. Mother. Sister. Brother. A place. A room she returned to day after day. Midwest. Me, I had my costume and two days' growth of beard. I had to keep it that way for "matching" purposes. The beard. Not three days' growth. Not two and a half. But precisely two. The camera caught the difference. One of those "micro-budget" films, they call them these days, where you have no trailer to speak of, no privacy at all, so you end up wandering from one room in this cheap-ass hotel to another, where your costume hangs limply, lifeless on wire hangers, and yet another room where your books and toiletries rest. Wandering down long, stained, carpeted hallways, strangers appearing very small in the distance, then growing larger and more wary as you approach them, when they suddenly see that you really do look very scary in your two days' growth of beard and don't realize that you are just playing a character or are in the process of playing one and they believe in their eyes as you pass them that you might actually be the real psychotic thing and might do them real harm without even intending to. Just by walking past them. It even gets to where you actually enjoy scaring the hell out of strangers on your way to breakfast. Getting closer and closer to them down the long, stained hallway and refusing to take your eyes away. Refusing to dodge them. Pinning them, in fact, between feeble attempts to smile cordially in the polite American morning manner or ignore you altogether as though you were just another cockroach in the system. It does no good to tell yourself that the whole grim event will only last three more weeks, like some kind of prison sentence where you cross off days on a makeshift calendar. Xs through numbers. Days clicking. A wall of rough concrete.

I find myself now, becoming suddenly enraged. A surge comes over me. Maybe it's some serious entropy to do with the inevitable deterioration of brain and mind. Maybe something like the madness of Otis in the 1700s standing at his open window, hands clasped behind his back, staring down into the dark wet grass of the Commons, picking up a flintlock pistol from a delicately carved French end table and firing it into the Boston night. Maybe it's like that. The Brits remain in rigid formation—eyes straight ahead, jowls firmly set, oily black bear fur hats, and their boots all polished.

Anyway, my plan was to carefully build a character, drip by drip, in the sense of sediment—the way it sometimes drifts to the bottom of a glass of river water before you take a cool long drink. It didn't happen, of course. There was nothing "careful" about it. I don't know what I was thinking.

I had room 329, ground floor, looking directly out at the stagnate waters of a small Hudson tributary. The town itself was conceived in the mid-1600s, burned and pillaged by the British in 1777, and littered with Dutch stone "rubble," structures for grain deposit. This pathetic, side-of-the-road motel was built along the lines of a traditional Holiday Inn, lacking the slick green plastic veneer and welcoming marquee for deer hunters. Remodeling from twelve-by-twelve scaffolding took place daily. Construction workers in yellow hard hats and steel-toed work boots came and went from the restrooms marked "For Handicapped Only," trailing hunks of plaster and dust. There was no laundry service, no restaurant. A potato chip machine that took several quarters, and one maid with a Latvian accent who never entered your room unless you hung a "Please Change the Linens" sign on your doorknob. Strings of gray junk hung like mushroom spores on the air conditioner's grill. Black plastic boxes filled with rat poison nesting in the long weedy grass outside the window.

The very first element I snared for sure in my "character search" was "exile." The sense of being "apart" as a way of life. How it comes to pass that a human is set adrift. Something intimately familiar. I was at it again. The Blackmail Girl seemed to have disappeared completely—fallen into the abyss. Most likely my inattention—lack of texting. Lack of feeling sensitive. I imagine. I don't know. I had this in me. "Exile." I knew it. There was no need for preparation. My whole life was a preamble.

Happenstance

"So you want me to believe that my miniature dead father visited you in a dream and asked you to thank me for allowing him to get a breath of fresh air?"

"I don't want you to believe anything."

"Are you just making this up?"

"Why would I do that?"

"To pique my curiosity, maybe. Cause me to think there's some symbolism involved—things might mean 'other' things."

"Don't you think everything does?"

"No. No. I don't, actually. I think some things are exactly what they are."

"What?"

"Just events! Happenstance. Circumstance. Chance encounters. Moments in time."

"'Happenstance'? That's an old-fashioned American word."

"You know what I mean."

"Do you think that's true of us?"

"What?"

"'Happenstance.' An accident?"

Maybe she got embarrassed. I mean, I would if I were her. Calling up and telling me she had been recording all our phone conversations! I mean, talk about a total violation of trust and confidentiality. I wouldn't even believe she was telling me that, at the time, it came as a complete shock. As though she had become an entirely different person. And then to turn the whole thing into a means of getting ahead in the world of fiction! What world is that? Still, I wondered about her. What was she really after?

What was I like at that age? Did I care what anyone might think? Did I care what anyone might wonder? What was I after? Putting out the garbage at Duke's Cube. The sun not yet showing itself. The garbage trucks whining away down the block. The cats running for cover. East on Bleecker Street, past the old Village Gate, past the Gaslight on the corner, across town. Tommy Turrentine carrying his trumpet in a paper sack. The black elms of Tompkins Square Park. Dripping smell of Polish soup. Mushrooms and barley. Windows steaming from the inside. Someone with a white apron mopping the floor. And the crosstown bus with the driver already singing a hit from *Porgy and Bess*. What was I really after?

Keep walking. Something will crack. Some break in the night sky. Keep the river on your left. That's her again, isn't it? Slipping away. Some little smear of light. All you can see is the now-and-then shine of blue steel, the now-and-then glimmer of four-sided spikes. When you look straight up you think you see bushes or hills or is it trees on either side. Or are they huge animals? Something sleeping. The tracks were right here. How could I lose them? How could I be so careless? At the very least you should hear a train, don't you think? In all this space—nothing to stop the sound. It should be on my right by now. I hope she's gone when I get back. It should be on my right by now. I hope he is too, tell you the truth. Stop seeing imaginary things—beings, imaginary beings. That's it! Are they inside or out? How far have I wandered from the boardinghouse? I've never lost track completely. Like this. There's always been some guidepost, some sign, some rock, some stick. These beings seem completely indifferent to my progress. In fact I might just as well not be here at all as far as they're concerned. I've tried talking them into banishing me entirely—then at least I'd be rid of them. Excommunication. But they don't speak my language. They speak no language at all. They just hover and moan. Waver and blow. Like I'm not here at all.

———

I'd never been with a woman in that way before, especially an older woman, although Felicity was only about fourteen or fifteen at the time. She felt huge. I was lost in her body. Her breasts were immense and heaved like distant ocean waves inside her woman's bra, which she must have "borrowed" from her mother. The floorboards were rock hard on my knees. The rag rug had slipped away and I swam on top of her, flailing as though I'd never make it to the other side. She began scream-ing and making those same noises she'd made with my father the first time. I thought sure her voice might carry for at least twenty acres. Over the heads of grazing cattle, frantic lizards. Her eyes were squeezed shut and she took big fistfuls of my hair. I kept praying my dad wouldn't show up in the middle of all this. After days of her waiting for him, he finally shows up in the middle of all this! It was unbearable to imagine! I rode her like a pony trying to stay on. She slipped away, grabbing me between the legs and shoving me into her. It was an incred-ible mess. Cum all over the place. She jumped up suddenly, gathered all her clothes, and ran out the front door, half naked, then turned on the porch and ran back in, and got on top of me. I was still stretched out, bewildered. I thought she was going to crush me. The sheer weight of her. Her pelvic bone. I thought it was all over and here she was on me again except worse—more savage, more huge. Her mouth opened and I saw tiny animals escaping: tiny animals trapped inside her all this time. They flew out as though something might catch them and drag them back into imprisonment. I could feel them land on my face and crawl through my hair, searching for a hiding place. Each time she screamed the animals flew out in small clouds like tiny gnats: little dragons, flying fish, headless horses. They came tumbling out, scratching at each other. The amazing thing is that I stayed hard all this time. Even after ejaculating all over. I was hard as a stone salute. That must've been why she returned.

I avoided my father after that. I could see him at dusk in his rocker with a glass of whiskey and a glass of milk beside it, picking the shrapnel scars on the back of his neck and staring at nothing from the front porch. I kept thinking he somehow knew about me and Felicity. That she'd told him in a moment of panic. That she'd suddenly had a spell of "honesty" and spilled the beans. That's why he was always staring off into the distance. It made no sense, though, that he hadn't attacked me right away—as soon as he'd found out. Why would he wait? He wasn't a man who carefully calculated his actions. If he kicked me out, where would I end up? Bakersfield?

These were the kinds of things I thought of as I wandered farther and farther from the house. As it turned to night I kept a bead on the kitchen light. I stumbled through plow ruts and tried to keep to the very edge of the fields so as not to disturb seedbeds or crops already heading out. Our sheep heard me coming and bolted off in a burst of gray away from the wire fence. I saw his bedroom light switch on and knew he was brushing his teeth with the glass of whiskey resting on the porcelain sink beside him. It was the same room in which I'd watched Felicity bouncing on the mattress. The same room in which I saw her throw the Mason jar. A pure white owl dove at a field mouse, snagged it, then flapped away into the dark. What would I ask my father if I had the guts? Would I ask him who he is? Who he pretends to be? Would I ask him what's on his mind? Does he "see" something? Does he "see" her and me? Does he think I might have fooled around with her behind his back? Got her hot and bothered? Caused those red blotches to emerge on her neck and face? Sweating. Caused her to drop her mother's underwear on the tile floor? Does he think I might be the one she really loves?

Tiny Man at the Beach

They are at the beach now. Carpinteria or Ventura—very bright and hot. The '49 Mercury is parked up by the highway, facing the pounding Pacific. All the windows are rolled down and the trunk is wide open. Salty air sweeps through it blowing sand against the whitewalls, half burying them. None of the miniature corpses are in evidence. Just the car—as though it has been abandoned in haste. No one's around. Just wind. Wind again.

Down on the beach, far below the cliffs, the miniatures are all lined up on their backs in the sand, as though taking sunbaths, even though they're all dead. Sea gulls circle above them, waiting for the chance to carry one of them off and tear it apart. The gangsters lie in a line right beside the corpses. They too look like they're taking sunbaths, but they're all still very much alive. Two of them have their shirts off and are applying baby oil to their dark olive skin. All the gangsters keep their felt fedoras on and all of them are wearing very expensive dark glasses, fashioned in Rome, with a brand name I can't pronounce. None of them wear sunblock. They're too proud of their Sicilian heritage to display white noses like a bunch of clowns in the circus. They've all taken their brogans off and their black silk dress socks. They wiggle their manicured toes in the sand and whistle at young girls strolling by. They call a group of girls over and show them the line of miniature corpses all on their backs. Taking the sun. The girls run away in horror, screaming, covering their noses, although the smell of death is very faint through the Saran Wrap. One of them runs toward the sea as though she's about to vomit. All the gangsters, in fedora hats, laugh hysterically and slap each other's high-fives so violently that one of them actually thinks he's broken his wrist. A black waiter shows up in a tuxedo and white gloves, driving an electric golf cart. They all order mojitos except one, who orders a vodka tonic. The black waiter jumps back on his electric golf cart after writing down their order, and heads off toward the clubhouse. You can just make out the roof over a distant ridge where a group of slender palms are swaying.

Mounds of Their Own Dung

The thing you remember most about feedlots is the smell—the smell way before seeing the actual cattle, usually Holstein crosses huddled in tight listless bands on top of mounds of their own dung. You imagine them sensing death—their future as frozen hamburger patties—but I could be giving them a prescience they don't possess. Mornings in the San Joaquin always carry a mist. Its origins are mysterious, because there is hardly any moisture to speak of. No water except for the placid irrigation ditches: the giant rainbirds dripping; white transportable Plasticine pipes at the edge of rows of lettuce. We used to call it "Tule Fog" when we worked alfalfa, loading trucks with square bales in the summer. That was farther south, though, down around Chino, where there was more green and it actually rained a little.

I put it in my head that I could walk the seventeen miles to the feedlot on the fifth straight day that Felicity showed up and was, again, asking to see my old man who was never there. I invited her in, as usual, out of the blasting sun, sat her down, as always, on the wicker chair, and poured the usual jar of iced tea for her. She sat exactly the same way she always did—with her back straight and her spine not being supported by the chair at all. She set the little black purse on the floor and balanced the iced tea, in the same way—on her knees, which were always pressed together and very tan. I made up some excuse to go back into the kitchen and snuck out the back, making sure the screen door didn't slam behind me. I ran for about a hundred yards, until my lungs ached, then walked in long strides down to Highway 5.

Meadowlarks trilled, then exploded out of a field of barley, landing on mesquite posts. Like Indians at the bus stop, they'd never look you directly in the face. Grasshoppers were everywhere and bottle flies would go smack in your eyes as though blind and suicidal. Crews of Japanese field hands were working strawberry patches in straw hats shaped like upside-down chocolate drops. A long line of giant bluegum eucalyptus marked the highway's shoulder and cast shade out into acres and acres of summer squash.

I started making up in my head what I'd say to my dad when I got there. A sort of little raggedy monologue as I marched my way toward the blur of occasional cars, on their journey up to San Francisco or down to LA in a straight line. "She's really desperate to see you, Pop. She wouldn't come every day if she wasn't. I mean—maybe you could just go down to the liquor store and give her a call. Or you could give me a message maybe and I'd tell her. Or a note. A note would even be better, wouldn't it? She'd see you'd signed it and everything. It would almost be like talking to her. Maybe she'd imagine your voice even. Your face. As though you were actually talking to her. It might—I don't know, it might ease her mind or—it might even make her feel better about you. You know? The whole situation. I think she really likes you. She does. The way she talks about you. I mean—I can't stand it when she shows up looking for you and you're not ever there. I don't know what to do. I don't. I mean, I don't know what to do. Sometimes I try to talk to her but you know I'm not very good at that. I don't know what to do. I make things up. I do."

The hike to Coalinga was hot and dusty. I didn't even attempt hitchhiking. They never stop when they're going that fast, anyway. Occasionally, some old faggot insurance salesman. You can spot them right away. Driving alone. A bunch of suits and shirts on wire hangers behind him. His red balls hanging out his fly. I plodded on in the gravel ditch through disposable diapers, bottle caps, and used condoms. Crows and mockingbirds dotted the fence lines. Some guy in an old Massey Ferguson trying to be a "lone little farmer" holding out against the "Big Boys." Signs about water rights and how the politicians were to blame for the lack of it. White almond trees in full bloom. Boxes of bees pollinating apricots. Now and then a roadside fruit stand selling figs and watermelon. I could hardly wait to get out of this place.

I started thinking about how Felicity might have found us. How come she could have just showed up here in this godforsaken valley. It became clear to me that Felicity was what you call "underage," "jailbait," or whatever. Older men used to use that term, "jailbait." Something illegal like that or else they'd never have taken him away. The cops. My dad. We'd never have to have moved from that boardinghouse in the middle of the night like we did. He'd never have to have taken a job at the feedlot. He doesn't even know how to ride a horse, anyway. He just drives a pickup. Up and down the rows of cows, bawling and waiting for alfalfa pellets. Maybe that woman in the long pink coat was Felicity's mother and she had secretly followed us. I don't know why. Maybe the two of them have a place here. Somewhere in town. And the mother sends Felicity out here every day. Day after day. Like some kind of bait. "Jailbait," maybe that's it. Why isn't she in school, I wonder? It is summer. Not that her mother gives a hoot in hell about education. I can't see her grooming Felicity for some fancy girl's school back east or some Ivy League deal where they go on to "higher learning." Not that Felicity would want that kind of thing, anyway. I don't know.

When I finally reached the feedlot there was nothing but cattle and dust and a stench that made your eyes water. I couldn't see another human being. Miles of cattle. Black. Black and white. Red. Gray. Spotted. All kinds. All sizes. Flies. Shit. The air seemed like there might be a war nearby. That's what it felt like.

War and death. Mass graves. Desolation. Pogroms. No human beings. Nothing but the constant sound of cattle bawling as though their mothers were eternally lost. I saw a pickup truck, miles up one of the alleys. It would stop periodically. A man would get out and dump a bag of feed into the troughs, then run a pitchfork over the top of it as the heads of cattle poked through the pipes and lolled their long slimy white tongues over the green pellets. The man dumped the empty bag and pitchfork in the back of the pickup, then jumped behind the wheel. He'd go down the alley a few yards, then repeat the same process. I stood there for the longest time just watching. I had an impulse to wave, but I didn't. I saw the truck getting closer and closer but I somehow knew the driver didn't see me. I was sure it was my father. Who else would it be? I turned and walked away—all the seventeen miles back to the house. When I got back Felicity was gone.

Tiny Man Again

Two young girls with purple hair, silver nose rings, and no tops come strolling by. They are very proud of their recently oiled, firm breasts and permanently erect pink nipples pierced by golden safety pins. The gangsters all sit up in unison and pay close attention. They call the girls over and show them the miniatures. One of the gangsters, noticing the safety pins, asks them if it doesn't hurt. Both girls ignore him. The shorter girl kneels down in front of the line of dead miniatures and picks one of them up. She holds it in the palm of her hand. It's my father. Another one of the gangsters says, "Careful," but the girl starts unwrapping the Saran Wrap from around his head. The same gangster makes a move as though he's going to grab my father's corpse away from her but then he stops himself when he sees how gently she's doing this. All the other gangsters, with their fedoras on, sit in rapt attention. As the short girl peels away the plastic, the puncture mark from the dart stands out in a bright red dot on his forehead. She touches the mark very softly with the tip of her tongue, then re-wraps the head and places the tiny corpse back in line with the others. The girl then stands and brushes sand from her knees. The two girls hold hands and walk away. All the gangsters stand in unison and applaud as though at an opera but the girls keep walking. They don't look back. Far in the distance you can just see the black waiter cresting the ridge of the clubhouse, returning in his electric golf cart. All the drinks are jiggling, but you can't hear them at that distance. This is all I can remember. The imagery is beginning to fade.

A Grimace Is Not a Scream

Why or how he was shrunken inside those various dreams and apparitions is beyond me. Whether it was before or after his death on this earth was another question I had. Before his death, this is going back to '68 or '69, I'd say he'd already shrunk some around the shoulders and neck but this is also in accordance with the natural aging process. I mean that's what they always say about the aged, don't they? "He was once much taller, until that horse fell on him"—or—"He was once much fatter, until that woman who couldn't cook showed up"—or—"He was once much wider, until the river breached its banks." No matter. People will talk. It could be also that I'm dreaming him like that—tiny—because it's a way of distancing myself—but that's a bit Freudian, don't you think? As though there were some kind of outside intelligence driving all this—the subconscious or some such bullshit like that. Something I find hard to believe in. Why would I want to be distanced anyway? There's nothing I'm still afraid of. At least not from him, my father. Maybe it's his pain—his suffering. But why be afraid of his suffering? That's what I'd like to know. What's in it? For me, I mean. Hard to say what it was for him. Suffering, I mean. When you watch someone grimace or wince, what do you think they're feeling? It's certainly not a thing of pleasure that pops into your mind or happiness either. Neither of those. I mean, I suppose a grimace or a wince can mean anything up to a point, but do you necessarily have the wherewithal to really feel what the grimacer or wincer feels? Be that as it may. To be afraid of the sufferer's suffering is what I'm trying to discover. Is it even possible? Afraid of what? That the suffering might come over to your side? As though it's there already and watching the sufferer suffer only breaks open what's already lying dormant but rarely released. Or is it the impossibility of ever knowing? One thing's for certain: a grimace is not a scream and a wince is not a cry of anguish. But a miniaturization only causes you to look closer.

Felicity vanished. My dad walked the highway at night. Said he couldn't sleep but I know it was more about looking for her, hoping she'd show up. He hardly ever talked about it. In fact, he hardly ever talked period, just picked the scars at the back of his neck and stared at the fire. Every once in a while, he'd hear a change in the dogs and leap up from his chair and go rushing outside. The screen door slammed behind him as he stared out into the night and the dogs gathered around his knees, knocking their tails against the side of the porch. Hens clucked and fluffed their feathers from the shed where the tractors were parked and a cat scampered across the beam of orange night light cast from the creosote pole. He asked me again about the last time I'd seen her and I told him it was the time I went out to find him at the feedlot. He couldn't remember that time and I told him that was because I never actually talked to him, he looked so busy. "I'm never busy," he said, then he turned to the fire again and gave the log a little kick. Sparks flew into the room and lit up the wicker chair where Felicity always sat, waiting. For a second I thought I saw her but I was only dreaming. Sometimes it was like that out there at night, completely alone. Not even a neighbor's barn light. Just the two of us and the dogs.

I thought about Felicity—where she might have gone. Maybe she hadn't gone at all but just got bored with waiting around. Boredom was a real event in those days. What's going to happen? That's the question. What's going to happen.

Interrogation #1

"So, you claim to have never known this 'Felicity Parks.' Is that right?"

"'Parks'? No, sir."

"So, why then would her mother tell us that you do—you did? You *do*."

"Her mother?"

"That's right."

"She must be making something up?"

"You mean, concocting a story? Out of nowhere? Out of thin air?"

"I guess."

"She says this girl of hers—this 'Felicity Parks'—is fourteen years old."

"Is she? I don't know."

"How old are you?"

"Thirteen. Just thirteen."

"Just thirteen?"

"Yessir."

"And you haven't seen a girl like this wandering around your neighborhood?"

(The investigator shows him a photograph of "Felicity Parks" in a two-piece bathing suit, smiling directly at the camera.)

"No sir. Our neighborhood is very big, you know. Acres and acres. I mean—"

"Son, I've been the investigator for this county over twelve years. I was born and raised in Three Rocks. I guess I might know the neighborhood by now."

"Yessir."

"Don't get smart with me."

"No sir."

Thirty Acres of Dust and Snakes

I was disking the bottom field near the highway getting it ready for cantaloupe. About thirty acres of dust and snakes. I had a blue bandanna across my nose and my eyes and hair were filled with dirt. Behind the hot metal seat I kept an Army-green canteen full of water. I'd stop the tractor at the end of a full row, drop the bandanna down around my neck, and fish for the canteen while looking straight out at the highway, not really expecting anything new. When I first saw a flash of the long pink coat between the eucalyptus and the asphalt, it didn't really register. A piece of color—a flash of cardboard from a vegetable trucking crate, maybe. I pulled the canteen out from behind the seat without looking. Kept my eyes on the blank spot between the trees. Unscrewed the long cap on its little flat chain. Took about six big gulps of warm water. The tractor's engine kept popping in a rhythmic diesel monotony. I shut it off and the vast silence came swooping in. The slightest breeze moved long strings of silver eucalyptus leaves, dangling in dust, crackling faintly against each other. Then, I saw it again—stepping into the blank space as though by command, an apparition of the past—almost forgotten. The same woman—the same screaming woman from the boardinghouse. How old was I? "Cocksucking bastard!" That's what she called him. I can hear it. I can still hear it. Was it her? Hitchhiking? Her hitchhiking on an open highway? Miles from nowhere? They never stop for anyone. This river of traffic in between north and south.

I saw her sitting beneath one of the giant gums. Resting. Holding her right foot in her hands. Cradling it gently as though it were a dead bird dropped by the relentless heat. She would wet the finger of her left hand with her tongue, then gently caress the yellow blisters. The high heels lay to one side, covered in dust and the leather chipped in spots as though they'd been scraped against a rough plaster wall.

"This wouldn't of happened—wouldn't of happened at all if it hadn't of been for plain old disrespect. That's it—disrespect. Imagine a mother, any mother out here on the open highway, nursing her blistering foot—in the dirt! In the dust! When I should be having cocktails—gin and tonic—wined and dined at the Hickory Room. Not out here wallowing around like some kind of nasty roadkill. Like a squashed possum on the hot black asphalt. Disrespect! That's it—pure and simple. Some daughters ought to be stillborn. That's my opinion."

Interrogation #2

"Let me ask you something—what's your father do for a living?"

"Right now he works at the feedlots."

"Sorting?"

"Feeding mostly. Pellets—you know."

"How's he feel about you running around with an older woman?"

(*The investigator laughs lasciviously.*)

"I've never seen her before."

(*The investigator recovers from his "joke."*)

"Her mother's telling us that you have."

"She must be mistaken."

"You mean lying? Making up a story again? Why'd she seem so certain about it, then?"

"I don't know."

"She seemed very specific about where you and your father live. The color of your house. What your father drives. Time he goes to work. Things like that."

"Is she spying on us?"

"Spying? Her daughter's missing. She's looking for her daughter."

"Yessir."

"I told her to try and get a picture of Felicity at your father's place. A photograph."

"At our house?"

"That's right. I told her if she could do that then we'd have conclusive evidence. You know what that is?"

"Yessir."

"That means she can prove that her daughter was at your house. Hanging around. In black and white. 'Conclusive evidence.'"

"Yessir."

"If we can prove that then we know you must be the liar."

"Me? Why would I lie? I don't even know her."

"But you've seen her before?"

"No sir. I never have."

"How 'bout your father? Does he know anything about her?"

"No sir."

"Well, you can tell your father that we might be asking him to come in for a few questions as well."

"All right. I'll tell him."

"You can go now."

"How far back is it to my house? Do you know? How many miles?"

"You don't mind walking, do you? A young punk like you."

"No sir."

Burning Boats

I'm getting up in the dark lately, what is it—5:00 a.m.? Star-ing at the rafters. I've exiled myself without wanting to. I travel downstairs, holding on—down the circular staircase, to the kitchen. Everything's dark. Someone's been in here. I think it was me. Tangerine peels. Old tea. Open the back door to the stone porch. Outside, the yellow bulb struggles to glow through dead bugs. The raccoon has tipped the garbage can full of dog kibble over. Must've been that—the noise—the clatter. The single brick holding down the cover, cast across the porch. The lid, flung aside. Last night, I took a shot at this raccoon with my .410, point blank. Must've missed him entirely because here he is—back again. I can smell him but I'm probably hallucinating. A worse shot than that blonde. What was her name?

I'd like to call some girl, any girl—wake her up—but I know that won't do any good. What could she say? What would she do? She's in a different town, a different country, dreaming of other things.

I think I hear someone call my name. A woman's voice. Right outside the front door, loud and clear. What time is it, anyway? I go straight to the door and swing it wide open, almost dar-ing the invisible person to show herself. Nobody's there. Pitch black. I call out to whoever it was. No answer. The horses move along the fence line. I can hear their hooves through fallen oak leaves. They smell me. I slam the door. Nothing moves. The fire is out in the fireplace. Not even smoke. Not even embers. I can't start a fire at this hour. Someone must have been in there on hands and knees. Blowing. Lighting crumpled newspaper.

I go back to bed. Read about Viking burials at sea. Burning boats with dragon heads. Virgins scorched alive. Raccoon knocks the lid off the garbage again. I run down the circular stairs in my thick blue socks and load the .410. Time I open the back door, the raccoon's gone. A jet booms far off, in the dark sky. In the past. No sign of morning yet.

Interrogation #3

"Can you give us any good reason why she might have wanted to do away with herself? A girl so young as that?"

"No. Where was she found?"

"Just answer the question, please."

"Yessir."

"You have no idea."

"No."

"Abusive father? Mother? Alcohol? Drugs?"

"I have no idea."

"We understand that she was having an affair with a much older man."

"Really?"

"And also with this older man's son."

"An affair?"

"That's right."

"With the son too?"

"Yes."

"The two of them?"

"Yes."

"And where was she found?"

"Swinging from a bluegum eucalyptus off Highway 5. Southbound."

"Swinging?"

"Hanging from a small black pocketbook."

"Pocketbook?"

"Well—the strap."

"Must've been a long strap."

"It was."

"Must've been strong. The strap."

"It was."

"I mean if—"

"Could we continue with the questions, please?"

"Yes—I just wanted to ask when you found her."

"That's not pertinent."

"No."

"Your father—does your father still live out there?"

"Out where?"

"Off Highway 5. Near the lemon groves."

"As far as I know."

"You haven't seen him for a while?"

"No."

(Long pause, in which the investigator clears his throat, has a glass of water, rustles papers, adjusts reading glasses, cleans them with a Kleenex, stares out the window at acres and acres of parched land: dead almond trees all lined up in perfect rows. Another long pause, in which the person being questioned suddenly feels an overwhelming urge to take a huge dump.)

"Excuse me, but is it possible for me to use the bathroom?"

"Of course—turn right outside the glass doors, then a sharp left. Just follow the signs to the bottom of the hallway. It'll be on your left."

"Thanks so much."

"Not at all. Here's the key."

(The investigator holds out a giant Ping-Pong paddle with a letter M *in black electrician's tape stuck to it. A skeleton key hangs from the handle. A policeman in an everyday police-man's uniform takes a step forward.)*

"Officer Barnes will help you with the handcuffs."

(Down the long hallway with murky murals of conquista-dors, Indians, and gold miners. Officer Barnes keeps right on his heels but never speaks and never touches him until they reach the men's room door. He has the creeping sense that Barnes is about to jump on his back like a gigantic vampire bat and suck all the blood out of his neck, but he doesn't. When they finally reach the men's room door and stop, Barnes unlocks the handcuffs and, surprisingly, allows him to enter by himself. He discovers the quickest way out—through an aluminum vent high above the yellowed latrine.)

Eye to Eye

They came looking for him at his father's place and the father told them he hadn't seen him. Ran off and joined the circus or some such nonsense. Told them the two of them had never seen eye to eye about anything anyhow. When they asked him about Felicity, he didn't know any "Felicity." When they showed him Kodak snapshots of Felicity sitting on his lap in a rocking chair, dangling her tan legs and her Western boots with tiny pistols carved into them, he told them the pictures must've been "touched up." Told them that he'd known other guys who'd had that done down in Mexico just to show their friends they weren't a faggot and that they really did have a good-looking girl tucked away somewhere who really did love them. The cops all laughed and, secretly, admired and liked him even though they knew he was lying. They officially arrested him when they discovered a blue lace bra that opened in convenient horizontal slits around the nipple area. They searched everywhere until they finally found it tucked under a sheepskin rug beside his bed. My dad told them it must've been put there by someone who wanted to frame him. When they asked him who that might be he told them it was probably me, his own son, who wanted to get back at him for one thing or another. When they asked him if his son held some kind of a grudge, he said he had no idea, except he always felt that I had it in for him.

I follow her trail. Again. There are remnants caught on cactus. Shreds from her shorts, pieces of hair. I get excited. I can feel that throbbing high in the throat. Something in the head booms. The chase maybe? The breath quickens. An impression of bare legs churning. Powerful thighs. Tan. Never slacking pace. Young. Tan. What is she thinking? Why has she come back? The mind won't stop. No matter what. The thought tripping over itself. Appearing, disappearing. Her future. Must be. She's so young it's got to be her future. Why would she ever take a dip into the scary past? Something she sees up ahead. Tangible. A picture. Maybe more men. She has no idea I'm right behind her. Or does she? Did she plan this out? Is she actually leading me to my own disaster? Am I? (Don't get paranoid. It's midday, for Christ's sake.) Maybe that's her muddy step, right there. But it hasn't rained for thirty days.

I went back there to the place where that investigator guy said they'd found her—swinging by the neck, from a bluegum. I walked up and down that whole stretch of dust looking up into the millions of skinny leaves clattering around in the highway wind. Traffic on 5 poured past me on the left and the right. She was nowhere to be found, of course. No sign of her. Not even the black purse strap that seemed to have held up so well. Nothing. They'd taken her away—everything. Probably in one of those body bags. Probably ashes by now. I did find the tree though. I'm sure it was. It seemed to be much older than the rest. Tired. It was like it had seen too much. Rooted in the same spot for all those years. Branches all gnarled up like goat knees.

There was one branch that had little desperate scratches on it—almost like something might have chewed it in the night. Some rodent or bat. Tiny little teeth marks the size of a child's, just cutting molars. Whatever it was, it was after something sweet. Something under the bark. Eucalyptus and Vaseline? I remember my mother coating my chest with that. It made your eyes water.

A Note About the Author

Sam Shepard is the Pulitzer Prize–winning author of more than fifty-five plays and three story collections. As an actor, he has appeared in more than sixty films, and received an Oscar nomination in 1984 for *The Right Stuff*. He was a finalist for the W. H. Smith Literary Award for his story collection *Great Dream of Heaven*. In 2012 he was awarded an honorary degree from Trinity College, Dublin, Ireland. He is a member of the American Academy of Arts and Letters, received the Gold Medal for Drama from the Academy, and has been inducted into the Theater Hall of Fame.

A Note on the Type

This book was set in Caledonia, a typeface designed by
W. A. Dwiggins (1880–1956). It belongs to the family of printing
types called "modern face" by printers—a term used to mark the
change in style of the type letters that occurred around 1800.
Caledonia borders on the general design of Scotch Roman but it is
more freely drawn than that letter. This version of Caledonia was
adapted by David Berlow in 1979.

Typeset by Scribe, Philadelphia, Pennsylvania
Printed and bound by Berryville Graphics, Berryville, Virginia
Designed by Iris Weinstein